LTURE

ıer with
o finish.
e, holding
up her arm for him to see.
There was a crazed gash down the inside of it and the blood was already pouring freely from the wound. She put her other hand across to try and stem the flow, but the blood bubbled thickly through her spread fingers. Herne looked coldly at the wall-eyed man. 'You got three seconds to drop that bottle and go for one of them guns," he barked . . . '

Also in this series

HERNE THE HUNTER 1: WHITE DEATH
HERNE THE HUNTER 2: RIVER OF BLOOD
HERNE THE HUNTER 3: THE BLACK WIDOW

and published by Corgi Books

John J. McLaglen

Herne The Hunter

4: Shadow of the Vulture

CORGI BOOKS
A DIVISION OF TRANSWORLD PUBLISHERS LTD

HERNE THE HUNTER 4:
SHADOW OF THE VULTURE

A CORGI BOOK 0 552 10431 0

First publication in Great Britain

PRINTING HISTORY
Corgi edition published 1977

This book is set in 10/11pt Plantin

Corgi Books are published by Transworld Publishers Ltd.,
Century House, 61–63 Uxbridge Road,
Ealing, London, W.5.
Made and printed in Great Britain by
Hunt Barnard Printing Ltd., Aylesbury, Bucks.

This is for Angus Wells: he writes westerns too.

1

Jed Herne shifted his weight uneasily from one booted foot to the other. He hadn't felt so damned awkward since his ma had made him go off to his first ever barn dance wearing a brand new pair of pants. Or since he had gone calling for Louise that first evening . . . a bunch of flowers pushed down behind his back. It had been a warm evening, he remembered, but the hand that held the daffodils had been fixed and cold.

His Louise – his Louise that was. That had been. Had been his until the night he hadn't been able to get back through the snows to their homestead . . .

But seven others had. Seven men. They had killed the wife of his nearest neighbour. Then they had raped Louise. All seven of them. Until every orifice of her body was running over with their lust. They had not bothered to kill her. Simply left her for Herne to find on his return.

They had not needed to kill her: she had done that herself.

Jed Herne closed his eyes for an instant. Imprinted sharply upon the back of the lids was the memory of her body. Swinging. Swinging slightly at the end of the rope she had tightened about her own neck.

Seven men. He had chased them, tracked them down like the vermin that they were. He had seen that they paid. That they died. Even to the last he had enjoyed it. He had stood over the body of that young boy and fired bullet after bullet into him from such close range that his body had been torn apart. Only when his gun was empty had he stopped.

Now that all seven were dispatched to the shades of Hades,

did that mean it was the end? An end? He didn't know. C not be sure. But he suspected that it was not.

Herne's thoughts were interrupted by the sudden bello a ship's horn and a voice shouting.

Then she was standing in front of him, her head held to one side inquisitively. She had on her best new dress and was carrying a parasol in her left hand. In her right she held a square-shaped leather bag. The rest of her belongings had been taken on board earlier.

Herne looked at her and observed, as he had done many times before, how beautiful she was. How beautiful she had become since he had taken her with him on his quest for revenge. A beauty that disturbed him greatly.

He felt as awkward as he had that first time standing before his Louise. Only this time he didn't have any flowers and he wasn't courting. He was seeing Becky off on the journey to England where she was to go to school. She was just fifteen.

'What is it, Jed?'

'Nothin' special.'

Her eyes didn't believe him.

'I was thinkin' you're goin' to be pretty cold on that ship with only a dress on. Hell, it's December. Just 'cause we're having some freak sun, don't make it summer.'

Becky smiled. She knew that whatever it was he had been thinking about, it certainly hadn't been the weather.

'Don't fret, Jed. I've got my coat in the cabin. I'll put it on just as soon as we sail.' She paused and took a step towards him. 'They've been calling out for everyone to get on board. I shall have to go.'

'Sure.'

Becky took another small step towards Herne. Right up close to him.

'Aren't you going to kiss me goodbye, Jed?' she asked, head upturned and eyes staring into his.

Jed reached out his hands and placed them on her arms. Through the thin material of the dress, she could feel the strength of his broad fingers. He squeezed her and moved his face down over her own. She slid her body between his arms and he kissed her gently and quickly on the cheek. She was aware of the roughness of his skin, where his beard had already begun to push through despite his morning shave.

'Jed?' Her voice sounded strangely loud, unnerved. 'Jed?' She said his name again and the tremor was even more pronounced.

'I shall miss you, Jed. More than . . . more than . . .'

Herne was certain that she was going to break down in tears and prayed to heaven that he was wrong.

She was looking at him: her face still very close to his own.

'Goodbye, Jed.'

And she kissed him. On the mouth. One moment her soft, cool lips were pressed against his, the next she had wheeled away and was running towards the foot of the gangplank, her bag and parasol bouncing clumsily at the end of either arm.

She was unable to wipe away the tears.

Herne watched the girl's shapely figure as it moved along the deck and heard the shouts of the sailors as the gangplank was hauled up and final preparations for moving off were made. He lost sight of her for several minutes, then she reappeared, one hand clenched round the rail, the other waving.

He lifted his arm and waved back. Once only. As positive a gesture as he could make it. Then he turned and walked away from the dockside.

He knew that it would be possible for him to remain there until the ship's sails were no more than white shadows on the horizon and Becky's waving hand a gull's wing on his imagination. But that was not what he wanted. He had never liked saying goodbye.

A man who lived as Herne did, by his gun, couldn't afford to let the past get in the way of the present. If you were faced down in the street by a young punk kid with a sixgun strapped to his side, you couldn't afford to have some damned memory come creeping up and tapping you on the shoulder.

Besides, he had his gutful of memories already.

The street that led away from the docks was straight and as he walked along it, Jed Herne never turned round once.

New York! Herne mentally cursed the place and spat down into the gutter. Down by the docks it had been squalid and foul. The wharf buildings ran with rats, even in the daytime, and the stench that wafted out from between the cracks in their scarred wooden walls hit you in the face like the smack of an ugly, open hand.

But maybe, thought Herne, just maybe, that's preferable to being uptown surrounded by . . . by all this.

He looked across the broad cobbled street at the four and five storey buildings that stood squatly in their places, each as hard, as unyielding as its neighbour. They were nobody's homes; places of business. Places where men went each day and thought up schemes for making more and more money so they could build more and more of those damned brick hells!

Herne longed for the open space of the prairie and for a horse beneath him. He would give the animal its head and let it take him where it chose. Together, they could ride for ever and never run out of room.

But here. For all the width of the street, Herne felt cramped, threatened. He looked up at the sky and as he did so a cloud ran its grey edge over the December sun.

Herne braced his back against the sudden cold. He crossed the street, heading back for his hotel. He would collect his things and get out just as soon as he could.

The hotel was a three storey building with a lot of brass and gilt downstairs in the lobby and torn and soiled sheets upstairs on the beds. Not that Herne was too worried by that. It had been a long time since he had slept under anything other than the old blanket he kept rolled up behind his saddle.

Herne felt in his pocket and pulled out a handful of coins. He was wondering whether he could afford a drink. Hell, he needed a couple of drinks! Only paying a term's fee for Becky's schooling as well as for her passage across to England had taken about every dime he had. Still . . . he flipped a coin up into the air and caught it smartly . . . he guessed that a shot of whisky wouldn't make that much difference.

He was half way across the rich red carpet when he noticed the man in the dark suit. He was certain that he'd seen him before, standing around the dock side.

Jed ordered his whisky at the bar and watched the man in the mirror. It was one of those with an artist's impression of a naked woman painted on it in gold outline. The man's head was filling one of her breasts.

Herne turned slow and easy, conscious that his Colt .45 was upstairs in his room, wrapped up carefully and stashed away in his bag. All that he had was the honed bayonet blade which he carried down inside his boot. He shifted the glass over to his left hand, lowering his right shoulder so that the fingers of that hand swung loosely above the top of the weapon.

The man in the dark suit looked directly at him. He was younger than Herne, but not by many years. His face was pale, as though he had never exposed it to the sun, almost as though he had lived permanently in the shadows. The man's head twitched – the same odd way it had done the time Herne saw him by the dock side. That's how he had remembered seeing him before. The man stood up – he was about six feet tall and Herne could detect, beneath the well-tailored clothes, the firm outline of muscles that he suspected the man knew how to use. And underneath the flap of the jacket . . . ?

Herne tensed as the man's right hand hovered around the pocket of his coat, then darted inside, removing the single button from its neatly threaded hole.

His gun belt was clearly visible. Herne's right arm dipped lower, the man's eye following it down. He stared piercingly at Herne for several tense seconds then turned and walked away.

Herne watched him go, making sure that he was well out of sight before turning back to lean against the bar. As he finished his drink he kept his eyes on the mirror. But there was nothing to see: just his own reflection and a painted, naked lady.

He drained his glass, enjoying the roughness of the alcohol as it burnt against the back of his throat, then moved easily over to the desk and collected the key to his room. On the first flight of stairs the sound of his boots was muffled by the pile of the carpet. After that, there was nothing but bare board and the noise of leather on wood reverberated around him.

If there was anyone up there waiting it would give them plenty of time to get clear . . . or to move back into hiding. Herne stood at the end of the landing, facing towards his room. There were three doorways on either side before his own. The corridor was poorly lit.

Herne walked carefully, slowly, every muscle tensed and ready to react.

But there was no movement, no sound.

He unlocked the door of his room, stepped quickly inside and locked it again behind him. He picked up the bag and took out the wrapped gun, laying it down on the bed. Unwound the soft material and exposed the Colt. Oiled. Cleaned. Deadly.

He lifted it and rolled the chamber with the forefinger of his left hand. There was a metallic clicking sound. Perfect. He tested the balance in his hand. That was perfect too. It was part of him. An extension of his arm . . . of his brain.

There had been a time when he had set it aside. Had left it for a long time; tucked away in a drawer wrapped inside the same cloth that now lay unfolded on the bed. That had been for Louise. For her he had put up his gun. For her he had taken it up again.

Now it was all he had.

His heart missed a beat as he heard a footstep on the other side of the door. Not the sound of a man walking naturally. Someone who did not want to be heard. Someone who had not succeeded. Someone who was not smart enough.

Herne put one hand on the handle of the door, the other still gripping the butt of his Colt. He waited until he heard further movement, then quickly yanked the door open.

The man in the dark suit stopped in mid-pace. His legs were apart and his hands were empty. His eyes were staring down the barrel of Herne's gun and it didn't seem like they were too pleased with what they saw. The head shook more agitatedly than usual.

Herne gestured with the gun. 'Maybe you'd better step inside, friend. All this pussyfootin' around don't seem like it's goin' to be good for your health.'

The man did as Herne suggested. There was no way in which he was about to do anything else. He may not have been all that smart, but he wasn't a complete fool.

Herne shut the door and relocked it. He pointed towards the room's solitary chair. 'Take the weight off your feet. You bin doin' so much walking around, I reckon you must be tired out.'

The man looked for a hint of a smile on the westerner's face.

He didn't find one. Only two piercing eyes that seemed to look right through him.

'Now you're comfortable, why don't you unbutton that coat of yours?'

The man looked as if he was about to open his mouth in protest, until the Colt jabbed in his direction. He undid his coat.

'Now use your finger and thumb to ease that gun out of its holster and drop it down on the carpet. Take it careful, now.'

He did as he was told, never once looking at his gun as he did so, but still staring at the one that was pointing at him, with the broad thumb resting lightly against the hammer. Ready to cock it back in an instant.

'Right,' said Herne when the gun was on the floor between them, 'now suppose you tell me what the hell you're playing at.'

'Me . . . I . . . I . . . ' The attempt at an answer was lost in a series of jerks of the head. Herne was beginning to wonder if he might shake it plumb off.

'Keep your hair on, friend. I can't see no way you're goin' to get out of telling me what I want to know, so I should just sit as still as you can manage and let me have it.'

Again, since he wasn't a total fool, the man decided to do as he was told.

'I was hired to follow you. See what you were doing. Certain party seemed anxious to know if you was intent on leaving the country or not. I had to check on that. When it became obvious you was staying, I was supposed to find out what your plans was. 'S'far as I could.'

'That all?' Herne asked.

The man nodded. 'That's how it was. Didn't rightly know too much about it.'

'How come they hired you?'

His expression showed that he didn't know how he was supposed to answer, but he answered anyway. 'Got me an office here. Private detective.'

His voice swelled out with pride.

'You ain't from New York, though?'

'Hell, no. I'm from Mississippi.' The accent was becoming broader with each sentence he spoke.

'What you doin' in this place then?'

'Figured that New York was the place to come to get on. Make a name for myself. Make some money. This is where the money is.'

'And who's paying you yours?' Herne sat down on the edge of the bed and rested the Colt on his knee.

The man didn't answer. Herne asked him again. He still didn't answer. Herne raised the gun from his knee and pointed it at the detective's chest. The thumb went to the hammer and began to ease it back.

'I asked you a question,' he said, threateningly.

'Look . . . ' a shake of the head and a cough, ' . . . look, mister, you've got to understand, it's agin my code as a private detective to divulge the identity of one of my clients.'

Herne grinned. 'Well, I'll tell you something that you'd better understand and understand good. If my thumb keeps working its way back the way that it is, a point is goin' t'be reached where it won't go back no further. After that there's only one way it can go and that's forwards. If it does that then I reckon from this range it's goin' to splash a whole lot of your body all over your fine suit and over the walls of this hotel room too.'

Herne grinned again: 'You reckon you can understand that?'

The man nodded, frightened eyes fixed nervously on Herne's thumb.

'Right then, who hired you to follow me around? You goin' to be sensible and tell me?'

'Sure, mister. Sure. I'll tell you.'

'That's good,' said Herne and he let the hammer of the Colt slowly back down. He set the gun down beside him on the bed.

'See,' the detective began hesitantly, 'I had a wire from . . . ' He paused to shake his head yet again, then dipped his body forward in a sudden cough. Only the body kept on dipping . . .

His hand dived for the floor, aiming to scoop up the gun which he had dropped there. He moved fast and he had the advantage of taking Herne completely by surprise. Which meant that he actually got his fingers around the butt before something hit him hard in the left shoulder. Herne's boot. The impact was hard enough to send him rolling across the room and into the wardrobe that stood against the wall. But not enough to make him let go of the gun.

He bounced back and tried to level his arm. Herne dived on top of him, not wanting to use his own weapon if he could avoid it. His outstretched hands grabbed at the detective's forearm and forced it upwards, while his right elbow jabbed into his face.

There was a groan and a shout which was muffled by the same elbow coming in again. Herne squeezed the gun arm, pushing it away. Then he brought it down hard against the floor. Once. Twice. Three times.

Still the fingers would not loose their hold. Herne jumped up into a crouch and let go with his right hand, bringing it hard and fast across the detective's face. He stood taller, lifted his foot; brought the heel down on to the underside of the arm.

This time once was enough.

The fingers opened and let go of the gun as the man's mouth opened in a scream of pain. Herne booted the gun away and then booted the mouth shut.

He watched as the man crawled back and sat huddled against the front of the wardrobe, both hands held to his mouth. Blood was seeping down through his fingers and running under the cuffs of his suit and on to his white shirt. He pulled a hand away and spat. A gout of crimson splashed down on to the worn rug and something glistening white, probably a piece of broken tooth, came away with it.

Eventually he looked up at Herne, who still had not moved. When the nervous tic moved his head, he lifted a hand to still it and when that moved back to his mouth it left a dark red streak across the pale forehead.

'I'm waiting,' Herne growled. 'You said you was goin' to tell me somethin'.'

The detective looked at him. 'I can't, mister.' The voice was quieter than before, but in the stillness of the room Herne could hear him easily enough. The only other sound was the gurgling sound the man made when he breathed.

'The way I see it,' Herne told him, 'you don't have an awful lot of choice.'

'Mister, if it gets out that I've talked about a client, I'm never going to get another job.'

'If it gets out that you're dead, you ain't goin' to get too many jobs either.'

'You wouldn't . . . '

Herne didn't say anything. Just looked down at him. The man knew that he would. So he told him.

'It was this feller from the west coast. San Francisco. Senator, he reckoned to be. Name of Nolan.' He looked up at Herne. 'That name mean anything to you?'

Herne grunted. The name meant something to him, right enough.

'What you goin' t'do with me?'

'You take on anythin' else for Nolan? He hire you to do anythin' other than follow me?' Herne asked.

The detective shook his head emphatically. 'No. Just to tail you. Let him know by wire what you did.'

'What you aimin' to tell him?'

The detective thought for a couple of minutes then said, questioningly, 'That you caught the boat along of the girl?'

Herne nodded. 'Right. You do that and I'll reckon we're about square. That seem all right with you?'

'Yes. Reckon.'

Herne waited while the man made attempts to clean himself; he was going to walk down to the cable office with him to make sure the right message was sent.

'Hey, detective,' Herne said as they were walking along the street. 'What's your name, anyway?'

The man fished into his pocket and handed him a card. Herne looked at it: Tom Mitchell, it read, Private Detective. Then an address.

'You got any kin?' Herne asked him.

'Sure. Wife and a little boy.'

'What do they think about this job of yours?'

Mitchell shrugged his shoulders. 'Sometimes she worries 'cause I'm out of the house a lot, but mostly she seems to like it okay. It's a good line of business and things are picking up all the time. I reckon that if things carry on the way they 'pear to be, it might become a regular family business. Why, be good to have my son take over from me when he grows up. Somethin' to make a man proud, that would be, don't you think, mister?'

But Herne did not reply. He was thinking, though. Thinking about the son that Louise had lost the second it was born . . . and about the child that had been alive in her womb until . . . until those seven men had trudged, drunkenly, across the snow to her cabin.

And one of those men had been Senator Nolan's son.

Herne had exacted his deadly revenge on Nolan's son first of all. Since when the aged Senator had sent several men chasing Herne in an effort to get him gunned down. None had been successful, though one, Whitey Coburn, a former friend of Jed's, had come mighty close.

Maybe this was a chance to get Nolan off his back. At least with Becky in England he'd not endanger her life.

Herne studied the cable and gave it back to Mitchell, who folded it neatly and pushed it down into his pocket.

'You goin' to leave it at that?' Herne asked him.

'Sure. You got my word.'

He held out his hand and Herne took it. It was a strong hand and it gripped his own firmly.

The two men walked together as far as Herne's hotel. Herne stepped into the lobby and the other man walked on, heading back for his wife and son.

Hell, thought Herne, she can tend to that cut mouth of his and treat him like a wounded hero, while all I've got is four blank walls and not even enough money to buy some more whisky. Not if I'm going to get any kind of train ticket out of here in the morning.

He sat in the chair for a while but the thoughts which kept running back and forth through his mind disturbed him. So he pulled off his boots and most of his clothes and clambered into the bed. After a few minutes he got up again and fetched the Colt from his holster on the belt that was slung over the back of the chair. He laid it alongside the edge of the pillow and closed his eyes.

All he wanted was morning and the first train that headed back west.

Even in the midst of the city, Jed Herne's internal alarm clock worked to perfection. Just as the dawn was breaking on the skyline, he rolled over on to his side and was awake. In the midst of that action, his hand had reached the short distance to the butt of his Colt.

Herne blinked his eyes twice; sat up; rolled his legs over the edge of the bed and felt his feet hit the floor; stood up; shook his head; coughed; spat the tight ball of phlegm into the china bowl on the wash-stand; stretched his arms wide; yawned.

Then he put down the gun and began to get ready.

During his brief preparations Herne considered whether he should strap the gun on or not. He decided against it. Too many questions might be asked here in New York. He would stash it away and wait until the train had left the city far behind.

Not many minutes later, he turned the large key firmly in the hotel room lock and moved into the corridor. Less than half a dozen paces along, towards the top of the stairs, he heard a door open behind him.

Jed threw himself flat, right hand clutching automatically for the gun that was not there. Rolling fast, he saw a flash from the door at the end of the corridor and heard the sound of the shot fill the space between himself and the man who had fired.

He covered this space as quickly as he could, his hand reaching lower this time, diving down for the weapon concealed in his boot. The room door slammed shut just before he reached it. Herne kicked hard. He pushed himself back against the wall, waiting for the bullet which he knew must come.

Bayonet gripped firmly in his hand, he dived for the opening, sending his body rolling into the room. Another shot echoed round the room, but by now the man was panicking badly. Herne came up into a crouch, bringing his right arm back behind his shoulder.

Mitchell stood in front of the wardrobe, mouth partly open,

his gun pointing downwards. His head began one of its nervous little shakes: it never finished it.

The blade of the bayonet pierced the side of his neck, a couple of inches below the jawbone. Pierced it and went right on through, holding him tight up against the wood.

Herne stood to his full height and watched as the fingers of the detective's right hand spread themselves outwards with agonising slowness until finally they let the gun fall to the floor. He walked over and caught hold of the handle of the bayonet and pulled; it took a hard tug to free the point from the wood, but once done it eased smoothly through the flesh.

Herne stepped back a pace as Mitchell's body seemed to hesitate about falling. As though eventually realising there was no longer anything to hold it up, it folded over on to the carpet.

Herne cleaned the blade of the bayonet and replaced it inside the sheath he had had built into his boot, then began to go through the detective's pockets. He found the copy of the previous day's cable. And another . . .

A cable had gone to Senator Nolan early on the morning of that same day. In it Mitchell had given full details of the school to which Becky was presently sailing.

Herne stared at the slip of paper with dismay. He realised that if Nolan knew where the girl was and if he found out the second cable was a lie – as now seemed likely with Mitchell dead – there would be nothing to stop him making an attempt to get his revenge on Herne through Becky.

He had known from the start that having the girl tagging along was a liability. She hadn't meant to, but she had hamstrung his movements when she was with him. Now she was going to do the same from the other side of the ocean. Unless . . .

Herne screwed up the piece of paper and let it drop to the floor. It bounced off the arm of the detective's suit and rolled along his chest until it became stuck down in the blood that was still streaming from the gash in his neck.

'Too bad,' said Herne, 'you should have stuck to followin' folks around . . . not that you was much good at that.'

He looked down at the pale face – even paler now. It had been a shame that he had been forced to kill him; he had even begun to like the detective in a funny sort of way. What the hell was a person like him doing taking out a contract on Herne's life? He could guess at his orders: if he sails, let me know where for – if he doesn't, then get rid of him before he leaves New York.

'You're a fool, Mitchell,' Herne said to the dead man. 'A fool who was just too damned greedy. Probably thought it would be somethin' extra for that wife and kid of yours. And now all they've got is a blood-stained suit an' a dead man inside it.'

The detective had stood no chance. If Whitey Coburn had not been able to kill Herne, then Mitchell wasn't even worth entering for the race. Not that Nolan cared about that. He didn't mind how many lives he bought with his money and then threw away again. When you had that amount of money, lives were cheap.

Herne knew that Nolan wouldn't stop wasting them until he had got the revenge he wanted. There was only one thing left for him to do: he would have to kill Nolan himself. And how many others on the way to him?

Jed Herne sighed, turned and left the room. Killing never stops, he mused.

2

It was cold in the train. Cold and likely to get colder. Herne sat huddled back in his seat, rubbing his hands together to keep the blood circulating through them. At least he was out of New York, but this wasn't a whole lot better. Not yet, it wasn't.

He thought about the distance he was going to have to travel in order to reach his next goal. San Francisco. It meant travelling all the way across the country, from one coast to the other. Long. Difficult. Expensive.

As it was, he had only been able to buy a ticket as far as Kansas City. And that was less than half of the overall journey.

He knew that there were two ways in which he could get the money he needed to make the rest of the trip. He could stop off along the track and hire out his gun. It was something he had done often enough in the past. Hell, it was his past! Running money; riding shotgun; hunting men for bounty; fighting for the cattlemen against the sheepmen; for the sheepmen against the cattlemen. Using his Colt .45 for anyone who could pay the price that it fetched.

Only now he was getting old . . . old for a gunslinger . . . although his reputation lived on in some parts. Places where the mention of the name of Herne the Hunter still inspired awed expressions and somewhat exaggerated tales of his exploits. But most men would look at him now and pay him what they reckoned him to be worth on face value – and that was precious little. The big money would go to fresh-faced young punks who strutted around like turkey cocks, a pair of sixguns tied to their thighs and shiny black leather gloves with the ends turned back. Punks that Herne knew he could take before they had cleared leather.

But the men who were hiring out didn't know that.

So there was another way. Possibly better, certainly quicker. He could stake the few dollars he had left and try to win what he needed. There was usually a poker game or two on long journeys like this. Gamblers seemed to love playing on trains. It was even known, Herne thought sourly, for them to hire their own train especially for that purpose.

The train that had become snow-bound close to the Herne homestead, that had been a gambling train. The men who had got themselves drunk enough to tramp through the snow, they had been gamblers.

Eventually, thought Herne, they had lost.

But then, so had he.

He got up and, still rubbing his hands together, walked down the train.

There was a game in progress in the dining car. Four men playing so far; a couple of others hovering about deciding whether or not they should join in.

Herne stood with these for a few minutes, assessing what was going on.

They were playing five card stud. The dealer was a tall, very thin man of about forty. From the way he was dressed, Herne guessed that he would claim he was younger. He had a white shirt on, with frills down the front and on the cuffs. A dark blue cutaway coat over grey trousers. Although it was warmer in the dining car, Herne didn't think he could be all that hot. But he was the kind of man who would rather wear a shirt like that and suffer the cold than put on something less flashy and feel warmer.

He dealt the deck with professional flourish, giving each card a final, deft flick as it spun away across the table. From the size of the pot that was by his right hand, he was getting a good share of whatever luck was going.

Either that or his dealing was even more professional than the others realised.

The man who was losing fastest and heaviest was a good

few years younger than Herne and played with a kind of desperation which made his losing seem both more important and more necessary. He didn't shape up as though he had ever been a good player of cards and now he was getting so involved that whatever skill he might have possessed was thrown away.

The other two men looked as much part of the fixtures of the train as the seats and the cuspidor in the corner of the carriage. Short, balding, fiftyish; neither of them won too much nor lost too much; they just played the game as though the minute they stopped the train would stop also.

Herne looked at the loser. Sweat was starting to run down his face in lines which became darker and darker as they picked up the dirt from the journey which layered his skin. He was calling for cards in a voice that was altogether too loud. Making bets without calculating the odds with any intelligence. Pawing his cards greedily, like a child that is hungry.

Nothing that he did could disturb the dealer's rhythm. He just kept on dealing.

The loser wagered five dollars on a pair of sevens and looked astonished when it was beaten easily by the dealer's own hand.

Any hand would have been sufficient to break him: it just so happened that this was the one that did it.

'No!' He yelled and crashed a closed fist down on to the table top, close to the cards he had turned upwards the moment before. The cards lifted a little into the air, then fell back, sliding across each other's smooth surface as they did so. In the middle of the table, coins rattled and rolled against a heap of dollar bills.

Nobody moved. The man who had shouted stared across at the dealer, whose expression had remained unchanged. Poker players who know what they are about can control their faces in most situations; those who don't play well usually don't have any self-control either.

The younger man proved this point by hammering the table and shouting again. 'You bin winnin' and winnin' and winnin'. It ain't right! There ain't no way you could do that, time after time. No fair way!'

This time there was movement. Nothing sudden. Nothing that might send the scene too far too quickly. Those who were standing watching and who had been there when Herne arrived edged themselves away from the table. The two anonymous players began to push their chairs cautiously backwards, careful to keep their hands well in sight.

The dealer didn't move at all.

The young man looked wildly around him, appealing for some support and knowing that he wasn't about to get any.

'You bin playin' this game fer long enough. You all seen what the hell's bin goin' on here. This man's bin cheatin' us ever since we pulled out of New York. You gonna let him get away with it?'

His voice was high-pitched, strained. His eyes ranged round the assembled company in desperation. No one met his face; they looked at the floor, the ceiling, out through the window at the passing view.

'Well? You gonna let him cheat you out of your money or what?'

He must have known he was playing another losing hand, but with the fatal drive of a man who is born to lose, there could be no drawing back.

The train hiccuped over a bad link on the track and the piles of coins that had remained standing toppled over noisily.

The dealer brushed an invisible speck of dirt from the frill on the front of his white shirt and looked across at the man who was creating the disturbance as though he should be dealt with in the same way. His mouth opened lazily.

'It appears to me that these gentlemen have not been losing excessively. There is only one player in this game who has lost continually and that, sir, is yourself. I would have the temerity to suggest that the reason for that may be found in the fact that you are not a good player of the cards.'

The loser looked as if someone had slapped him in the face. He brushed away the beads of sweat gathering on his forehead with his arm. He looked very worried.

'Don't you . . . don't you . . . ! I bin playin' poker fer long enough to know what I'm doin'. An' I bin playin' long enough to know when I'm bein' cheated. An' that's right now!'

He lifted himself up into a half-standing, half-crouching position. The dealer looked at him coldly.

'Sir, so as there may be no mistake later, I would like to confirm what you have just said. You have accused me of unfair play during the course of this game. Is that correct?'

'You're damn right it is. Now you push that money back over the table to me an' I'll just go back to my seat and forget about the whole thing.'

He must have known the dealer would do no such thing.

'If I were to do that, sir, it would be tantamount to an admission of guilt on my part.'

'Don't you pull all them fancy words on me! That's all you are, a lot of fancy talk an' fancy clothes an' fancy dealin'. I bet you even shit fancy!'

'Whatever I do, I'm not intending to take any more shit from you.'

'Like hell you're not! You goddamn fancy cheat!'

He swung his hand down to his gun belt but opposite him Herne had his Colt clear of his holster and aimed at him before he had even had time to reach the butt of his gun.

'Don't do it, son.'

The man checked his move, staring at the drawn gun in amazement. The dealer remained seated. He did not appear to have made any move at all.

'So that's it,' the loser blustered finally, 'you got a fast gun workin' with you as well. Someone to back up your play when you git found out.'

'I haven't seen this man before today,' Herne said.

'Then what you doin' drawin' iron for him and agin me?'

Herne held the Colt steady. 'Never did like to see men throw their lives away for no good reason. Throwing away your money's different. There's ways of making more. Throwing away your life somehow just ain't the same.'

'You ought to stay out of things what don't concern you and . . .'

'All this gentleman has done, sir,' drawled the dealer, 'is to save your wretched hide. Though why he should think it worth saving is not at all clear. You will only throw it away again at the next convenient opportunity.'

The youngster stood up straight. He wasn't above five foot seven and he had a lean, hungry look which only emphasised his lack of stature. The dealer was thin by design; this man was thin by necessity. Herne wondered how he had managed to get the rail fare and what he hoped his journey would bring him. Wondered what he was running away from or running towards. If it was the former it was sure chasing him hard and if it was the latter, well that was going to keep shifting away from him the harder he ran after it.

That was the kind of man he appeared to be.

He looked from Herne to the dealer and back again. He could not cope with the gun of one, the words of the other. He was beaten and confused. His own gun was still in his holster but the gap between his hand and the butt of the gun was widening with every second.

Finally, he struck out at the table with his left fist and sent money and cards to the floor. Then he turned on his down-trodden heels and stomped out of the car.

Everyone sighed and exhaled loudly. The dealer turned and looked up at Herne. 'I thank you kindly, sir, for stepping in on my behalf. And I thank you on that young man's behalf for stopping him from getting killed.'

'You appeared to be taking things coolly,' said Herne.

The dealer allowed himself a smile and lifted his left arm up onto the table. He pressed the sleeve of the cutaway coat downwards on the surface and a spring released the concealed derringer into the palm of his hand. Herne looked at it, observing the intricate filigree work on the curved handle.

Not only a cool man, thought Herne, but a mighty dangerous one as well.

The dealer stood up and offered Herne his hand. 'My name, sir, is Pardoe, Wayne Pardoe.'

'I'm Jed Herne.'

'It's a pleasure to meet you, sir,' the gambler replied without showing any sign of recognising the name. 'Won't you join us for a game of poker? There appears to be an empty chair at the table.'

The initial stake that Herne had at his disposal to buy into the game had been so small that a few bad hands would have removed him from the table in the first ten minutes. As it was he began by winning more hands than he lost. He knew he wasn't an ace player, although his judgement was keener than most, and that he would need a whole heap of luck to keep him going.

Nobody in the game looked as if they were the type who made stupid errors although the dealer was the only one who looked capable of pulling off something exceptional in terms of sheer skill. It was a matter of staying in there and hoping that Lady Luck would smile down for long enough.

For the first hour, she stood behind Herne's chair and positively beamed down on his cards but then suddenly Herne found himself holding a pair of kings and a pair of queens and still losing out. He felt her protective fingers slip away from around his shoulders as she moved away and walked capriciously back round the table. There must have been something about the dealer's white shirt that attracted her.

An hour later everything that Herne had won had been pushed back across the table surface; from his diminishing pile into the central pot; from there to the dealer.

Herne found himself beginning to think along the same lines as the wild young man whose seat he had taken over. The gambler was having an awful lot of luck. Could he be dealing off the bottom, palming cards, using a marked deck? As if he guessed what Herne was thinking, the dealer asked the conductor to bring them a new pack. His luck didn't change.

The game continued. Herne bet his last two dollars on a hand with a pair of kings, and luckily picked up a third. Everyone was still in the game; the pot was large. If he was fortunate enough to win it, there would be enough to keep him playing for a lot longer. And then perhaps his luck would turn once more.

Herne looked down at the three kings in his hand. He wasn't about to throw them in.

He looked across at the dealer. 'Pardoe, you wouldn't care to take my IOU, I guess?'

The man smiled thinly and shook his head. 'Afraid not, sir. Rule of the game. Rule of my game.'

'Not a rule you'd care to bend?'

'No, sir. Not even after what you did for me earlier. But if you've got something you could trade in as a kind of collateral . . . well, I'd be privileged to accept that. If these other gentlemen are willing?'

He looked at them and they both seemed to nod simultaneously, although it might have been the movement of the train.

'Very well, sir,' said Pardoe. 'What do you have?'

Herne had been thinking about that very thing. The point was that he had very little. Only two things of any worth, in fact – his Colt .45 and his rail ticket. Everything else of value had gone towards paying for Becky's trip to England and her schooling.

There was no way in which he could part with the gun.

'Well, sir? We can't keep these gentlemen waiting for too long. Good fortune has a habit of going cold.'

In that December light which came dully in through the windows of the dining car, Herne thought he had probably left it too long already. But he was holding three kings.

He reached into his pocket and took out his rail ticket. He placed it down on the table. 'I've got this ticket for Kansas City. I guess that some of it's redeemable. I'll stake that to see you. If'n you're agreeable?'

The dealer looked down at the ticket, across the table at the other two players, who nodded once more. Then he called the conductor to check if the ticket was redeemable. It was.

'Very well, sir, I accept your bet. Now perhaps we should see what you are holding that makes you think it is all so worthwhile.'

They all looked at Herne's face, then down at the backs of the cards in his left hand. Herne turned them slowly over and spread them out in front of him.

'Three kings,' he said, needlessly.

'Beats me,' said one player.

'And me,' said the other.

Pardoe said nothing. He glanced up at Herne's face quickly

and somewhere around the corners of his mouth there was something moving that might have been the trace of a smile.

A smooth, manicured hand spread out the cards. Four queens.

One of the men sitting to the left of Herne whistled; the other began to say something, then stopped abruptly. There wasn't anything to say.

Jed Herne stood up and looked over Pardoe's handsome head to the conductor, who was standing behind him in the aisle.

'Well,' he said, 'guess I'll be leaving the train at the next stop. Whatever that is.'

At least they weren't going to stop the train right now and push him out into the middle of nowhere. Though Jed guessed that most any town between the Missouri border and Kansas was pretty much the middle of nowhere anyway.

On the other side of the window, the flat grasslands of lower Illinois were gradually being replaced by the hillier slopes of eastern Missouri. Hell! It was the wide open spaces he had been mourning for when he'd been back in New York. That was what he was going to get. With a vengeance.

A vengeance. He thought about Senator Nolan. Thought a lot of things about him and what he was trying to do. Ended up by thinking that he was still a hell of a long way off.

He looked round and saw Pardoe walking towards him. The gambler smiled briefly, then sat down opposite him.

'Game over?' Herne asked.

'Sure. Guess they decided they'd had enough. There don't appear to be many folk with a liking for cards riding this train. Perhaps things will pick up at Kansas City.'

'How far you going?'

The elegant shoulders shrugged. 'Depends on how the game goes. It always depends on that.'

'You always work trains?' Herne asked.

'Not always. Trains. Riverboats. Saloons. Anywhere there's a nice flat surface and men with money and a will to gamble, then I'll play.'

'You always do as well as you did today?'

The gambler grinned broadly. 'Guess so. Have to. Once I begin to lose then my living is gone.' He nodded down in the direction of Herne's holster. 'Much the same as you. The instant you lose out with that, your living's gone too.'

Herne nodded. Yes, if he lost out his living was gone, literally! He allowed himself a smile at his own joke.

'When you said your name back there in the dining car, I recognised it. You've travelled around. I've heard some of the things you're reckoned to have done. It all sounded very impressive. But I thought that was a while back ...'

His voice trailed away.

'It was,' Herne said flatly.

'You on a job now?'

'Not so you'd notice.'

Pardoe sensed that the conversation was over. He rose to leave. He was half way out of the seat when the youngster who had lost at poker appeared at the far end of the carriage. Only this time he was cutting back on the odds: his gun was already drawn.

The gambler stared in his direction and Herne turned his head so that he could see what was going on. Pardoe flashed him a look that said keep out of things this time. Then he stepped into the gangway between the seats.

Herne watched as the loser came slowly forward. The rivulets of sweat had reappeared on his face; the hand that held the gun was shaking slightly.

His mouth started to move but it was a while before the words formed. 'You . . . you took everything I had. My money . . . my . . . my . . . you made me look a goddamn fool in front of all those people. You and that gunslinging friend of yours. I bin thinkin' about it. I know there's no way I can let you get away with that. Just 'cause you got them fancy duds on and talk long words the way you do, you think that makes me nothin'. Well, I tellin' you that ain't so.' He glared at the gambler, whose eyes betrayed no sign of emotion at the hail of insults. 'You hear me, you bastard?!' He screamed.

'I hear you, son.' The gambler's voice was steady, cool as ice.

'And don't you call me "son". Who the hell you think you

are to talk to me like that? Hear me? Who in hell's name do you think you are?'

Pardoe studied the pattern of the carpet on the floor for a second, then gazed back into the youngster's face. 'Seems to me, son, that I'm the man who's going to have to kill you.'

'You're what? When I've got you covered this way! You ain't gonna kill no-one, mister, not for all your flashy clothes an' the rest. You're gonna give me back the money you cheated out . . .'

The words were cut short by the crack of an explosion. Herne, who had been watching the youngster, saw the sudden look of surprise on his face, then the blotch of red that appeared above his heart. As the blood from the wound spread, so the expression changed to one of pain.

By the time Herne looked back at Pardoe, the derringer had disappeared back up his sleeve.

'I was getting tired of his foolish babbling,' the gambler explained. 'I was going to have to kill him eventually.'

His words were punctuated by the sound of the youngster's body hitting the floor of the carriage. Hell, thought Herne, at last the poor son of a bitch had got what he was born for.

3

Jed Herne stepped down from the train. His boots hit the boards hard and the sound echoed along the short platform. Almost straight away the whistle from the engine swallowed up all other noise and the train began to pull out.

Herne turned his head and watched the train gather speed. A white frilled shirt cuff waved from one of the open windows. He gave a short wave back then started to walk along the platform. The station sign bearing the name of the town had been shot at by passing drunks and was dented and chipped but Herne could still read the single word: Charity.

Well, Jed thought as he walked through the wooden shack which was the ticket office, that sure is some name. Here I am without more than a couple of cents in my pocket; it's two days off Christmas – and I get put off the train at a town called Charity!

He stood at the top end of the street. It looked like it was the only street to speak of and it led straight down to the railway track. It looked like any other one-horse town in the mid-west. On either side of what for most of the year was a river of mud, ran a pair of raised boardwalks. There were only two buildings that rose above a single storey, the saloon and the bank. Otherwise, it seemed there were a couple of general stores, one doubling as a barber shop, an eating house, a blacksmith's and a saddlers.

Jed wondered where you went if you needed to get buried.

He also wondered what his chances were of finding some kind of work. They didn't strike him as being particularly high. Charity wasn't overrun with action. In fact, at that moment, the only thing active in Charity was Herne himself.

Had anyone been looking, he would have seemed an impressive figure. Around six feet two, weighing a little over two hundred pounds, he walked erectly, broad shoulders swinging slightly. His right hand was never far from the holster which carried his Colt. Every so often his fingers would brush the worn, smooth leather above the butt of the gun.

His face was strong and his eyes unwavering; the black hair hung down low over his collar – at the temples it had turned a handsome but tell-tale grey.

He didn't look like a man who had no job and nowhere to stay for the night. Though it might have been wondered why he hadn't bought himself a warmer coat, considering it was the middle of winter.

Herne stopped outside the saloon and looked up at the sign. '*Queen of the West.*' Above this was draped a piece of white cloth with the words, 'Rosie wishes all customers a Merry Christmas', painted in uneven letters along it.

He was tempted to step inside and return the compliment, but the knowledge that he couldn't even afford the price of a beer stopped him. He wasn't ready to join the groups of tatty bar flies and down-and-outs who spent their time begging drinks and scrounging for hand-outs from any lucky gamblers.

Instead, he wheeled round and walked back the way he had come. There was still no clear idea in his head as to what he might do. Perhaps if he walked down and chatted a while to the blacksmith, he might pick up some information he could put to good use.

But he did not get as far as the blacksmith.

The door of one of the general stores suddenly burst open and a sack of flour came flying out. It landed with a thud on a jagged edge on the side of the boardwalk. Its thin material ripped apart and the browny-white flour spilled out on to the hard surface of the street, filling the ruts and wagon tracks that were solid along its side.

Herne stood and waited. Something else had to happen. It did. There was a shout and a clatter and a pair of iron pans followed the sack through the door, striking the ground with a ringing sound that chimed strangely when they collided with each other.

Next to come were a side of bacon and a second flour sack, even larger than the first. It was pierced by the handle of one of the pans and its contents trickled out to join the flour that already lay over the street.

From inside the store came the sound of raised voices. Herne could only catch the occasional word, but even then it didn't sound too friendly.

As if to prove that, the next thing to come flying through the door was a body. A short, plump man wearing a striped apron left the store backwards and at a speed that suggested he sure wasn't coming out of his own accord.

He tried to keep his balance by hopping backwards, but after a few paces it was clear that he wasn't going to manage it. His arms began to flail wildly. His foot got stuck in one of the pans. He toppled backwards and hit the ground with a hefty thump which sent him rolling over into the flour.

Herne looked up from the sprawling, cursing, aproned figure to the man who had that moment appeared in the doorway. He was young; somewhere around twenty. His face was open and fresh, with a lick of fair hair hanging down between his eyes. He was wearing a thick plaid coat that Herne was immediately envious of. But he did not appear to be wearing a gun.

The man who was dusting himself down and trying to clear away the flour that was sticking to his face – he did have a gun. High on the left side and covered by the apron. It was there all right. There was no mistaking the bulge.

Nor was there any mistaking the anger in his voice when he shouted at the young man in the doorway. 'What the fuck do you think you're doin', you whippersnapper? No man throws Joe Brodie out of his own store and gets away with it. Least of all a nothing like you, Tom Newman.'

He hadn't moved for the gun yet, but it was obvious that he was thinking about it. Tom Newman must have been thinking about it also, but he did nothing to shift himself out of the way.

By now, Herne was not the only person watching. A good few had woken from their afternoon slumbers in the saloon and other buildings along the street and had staggered out into the dull light of the afternoon. A solitary, shadowy figure surveyed the scene from the window of the bank.

The storekeeper still stood there, flour covering his fat little body, yelling abuse up at the boy in the doorway. It could have been funny – except that someone was likely to get killed before many more words were exchanged.

'You had no right to throw my goods out into the street,' the young man was saying.

'What do you mean, your goods? Those things are mine, the property of my store.'

'Not any more they ain't!' guffawed someone in the crowd.

Brodie turned on him with a wild look which shut off his laugh like the firm wrench of a tap. The townsfolk obviously knew the storeman's temper and weren't prepared to run the risk of goading him any further.

'They ain't your goods since I bought them,' said Newman.

'If'n you bought them. Which you didn't.'

'I had ten dollars of credit with you and that's what I came here to use up.'

'I told you before, your credit ain't worth the bit of paper I've got it writ on. You got the cash, you pay me in that.'

Newman stepped down from the doorway and off the boardwalk until he was only feet away from the enraged figure of Joe Brodie. His clear face was set in its expression of anger. His blue eyes shone with an intensity that hushed the man's shouting for a few moments.

'You give me a credit note for that money the last time I was here. I come in today to redeem it. You know full well that I need all the cash I got in my situation. If my bill ain't worth the ten dollars you said it was a month back, then what is it worth?'

He glared at Brodie. The fat storekeeper glared back. Then his blubbery lips opened and he spat down at the ground in front of Newman's feet.

'That's what your credit's worth.'

Several people in the crowd began to snigger. Newman looked down at the greeny-yellow spittle that the storeman had dredged up from his chest.

'If'n you want it,' sneered Brodie, 'you'd better get down on your knees and lick it up!'

The young man sprang forward. Brodie did his best to get out of the way. He half managed it, but still took enough of the impact of the charge to get knocked to the floor. The two men rolled over and over. Brodie doing his best to pull the gun from underneath his apron. Newman concentrating on stopping him from doing just that.

The fat little man found the handle of one of the pans close to his right hand and grabbed at it. Newman saw it being lifted in the air and tried to intercept. He didn't succeed. The edge of the pan struck him on the forehead and set him flat on his back.

When he got back up on to one knee, blood was streaming from a wide cut above his left eye – and Brodie had managed to draw his gun. It was an old Navy Colt and it didn't look as though it had been fired for some time. The action would no longer be either smooth or quick. The aim would be a lot less than perfect. But from that range and against an unarmed man, it wasn't going to matter too much.

'I told you, Newman, you ain't worth no more than my spit, an' I'm going to shoot you down without thinking about it, 'cause that's no more than your due.'

Tom Newman said nothing; simply looked full into the fat man's face with clear blue eyes. The crowd that stood around held their communal breath. Brodie's finger started to squeeze down on the trigger.

'You got any last words you'd like to be remembered by?' Brodie asked. 'Any last orders you'd like to make?' His voice broke into a harsh, raking laugh. Then his eyes narrowed in their puffy cushions of fat.

'Nothing to say? Too bad. Too bad.'

'I got somethin' to say.'

The short, plump figure froze; the head swivelled round to the left looking for the new speaker. And found Herne. Standing slightly away from the rest of the crowd. Standing tall. Right arm curved away from his body. Fingers arched inches above the top of his holster.

'Who the hell are you? Who asked you to chime in here with your two bits' worth?'

'Guess nobody did.'

'Well then?'

'Well, it seemed like that young feller there didn't have too much to say for himself. And at a time like this, it seemed that someone ought to make with a few words.'

'What's the all-fired matter with you? You some kind of a preacher or something?'

Herne shook his head. 'I ain't no preacher.'

'What are you then?'

'Just a man who doesn't like to see somebody shot down in cold blood for no good reason.'

The fat face grew purple with anger. 'What d'you mean, no good reason? I got every reason.'

Herne shook his head again. 'That ain't the way I see it. What I heard makes that feller there the one who's got right on his side. If you give him a bill of credit, it only makes sense that he should be able to cash it in. Less there's other things here that you ain't talked about.'

Brodie's head twitched and he gave a hasty glance over his shoulder. He could have been looking in the direction of the bank, but he might as easily have been searching for a friend amongst the growing crowd.

Herne looked over the storekeeper's head. A lone figure still stood at the bank window.

'What you aiming to do then, stranger?' Brodie asked.

'I'm aiming to ask you to put up that old gun of yours, then help this feller to load what he wants on to that buckboard down there.'

Brodie leered at him in amazement. 'Is that all?'

'Not exactly. Those two sacks of flour will have to be replaced by new ones. And then you might apologise for your hasty temper.'

'I . . . I . . . ' But the man was rendered temporarily speechless. Which was more than could be said for the crowd, who were now talking excitedly among themselves. As for Tom Newman, he still had not made a move. But those blue eyes were blazing less fiercely now.

Joe Brodie had finally found his voice again. 'What you intendin' to do if I don't do like you said?'

'Mister, as long as you're waving that Navy Colt of yours around, I'm just liable to blow a hole right between those piggy eyes. Might let a little sense into that fat skull you got. Course, it'd be a mite late by then.'

The crowd chuckled.

'What's it going to be, mister? It's going to be dark around here soon and you'll be wanting to shut your store for the night.'

Slowly, grudgingly, the old gun was pushed down into the holster underneath the striped apron that was messed with dirt and flour. Brodie turned away, kicked savagely at the mostly empty sack closest to him, then walked up into the shop.

Tom Newman walked across to where Herne was standing and extended his hand. 'Mighty grateful to you, mister. You might have heard that old fool say, the name's Tom Newman.'

Herne accepted the hand in his own. 'I'm Jed Herne. Pleased to know you.'

'Jed Herne?' Newman said questioningly. 'Don't I know that name?'

'Could be. People some places got reason to remember it.'

Newman looked him up and down. 'I'll bet they have. Anyways, mighty glad of your help. There ain't anyone else in this place who would have done for me what you did.'

'You mean,' said Herne, 'that Charity ain't a good name for the place after all.'

'Hell, no! Couldn't be a worst one.'

Herne shrugged his shoulders. 'You going to be okay with him now?' He jerked a finger up towards the store.

'Yea. I reckon. But, look, I want to show how much I appreciate what you did there. You not only saved my life . . . ' He glanced down at the street. ' . . . you saved my bacon as well.'

Herne laughed. 'You don't owe me nothin'.'

'I do. And I ain't a man who likes debts. I should know about that, too. Thing is, I don't have a lot of money right now.'

'Seems a condition that's spreading,' said Herne.

'Maybe I could give you something. How about some of these supplies?'

Herne shook his head.

'Hell, Jed, I got to pay you back some way.'

Herne grinned and looked at the thick, plaid coat. 'You're not as broad as me, but that damn coat seems to sit on you with plenty of room. That might come in useful for the winter season. That is, if you got another one of your own at home?'

Tom Newman didn't waste time saying anything. He was already taking the coat off. He handed it over to Herne, who tried it on. It was a little tight across the shoulders, but apart from that it fitted him well enough.

And in his situation he couldn't afford to be fussy.

'Look,' said Newman, 'I live on a spread north of here. Only a small place. Keep it with my parents. Just about keep it anyhow. It would be an honour if you'd stop by tomorrow or the day after. Share what we got for Christmas with us. It ain't much, but what there is, you're welcome to.'

Herne reached out a hand and slapped him on the shoulder. 'Thanks, son. I'm not sure if I'll be staying on or moving through. But if I'm still here, well, I can't think of too many more places I'd rather spend Christmas than at your place.'

He turned and walked across the street. He didn't have any money yet but at least he had a warm coat. Things were looking up.

The sky was dark now and evening had almost settled over the town. Jed Herne knew that he was going to have to go into the saloon after all. Whatever his feelings about it.

Jed should have realised that in a place the size of Charity, what had taken place outside Brodie's store was going to be big news and it was going to travel fast. In Charity it was news if anyone crapped more than twice between sundown and sunup.

So that when he pushed open the batwing doors and walked into *The Queen of the West*, everyone was already talking about him. Which meant that as soon as they saw who had come in, all conversation ceased and the whole place became almost as silent as a graveyard.

Almost. There was the sound that Herne made as he walked

over to the bar and the clink of glasses made by the man behind it as he set them on the shelf.

By the time Herne had reached the bar, the talking had started again. Livelier than before and obviously directed at him. Nor need he have worried about scrounging a drink. Before he had had time to place his hand on the counter, half a dozen men had flocked around him, all anxious to be allowed to treat him to whatever was his pleasure.

Jed accepted a beer and a whisky, listened for as long as he thought necessary to their accounts of what had happened and how much they had enjoyed it, then made his way over to an empty table at the far side of the room.

He pulled up a chair and set the two glasses down in front of him. His back was to the wall away from the window. His eyes faced the front doors, with a view of the stairs to his right and the office door just beyond them. Anyone who came in or went out, Herne was going to have a good sight of them. He never allowed himself to sit any other way. Never had, even before he had heard how Wild Bill Hickok had got his. It was one of the reasons why Herne had stayed alive while others – his contemporaries – had not. One of the reasons. There was one more strapped to his side. Another tucked down inside his boot. The main one was underneath the mask of black hair. The grey at the temples didn't only testify to his age. It also meant he had lived long enough to have learned some sense. A whole lot of sense, compared with some folks he'd met.

He sipped at his beer, alternating that with an occasional slug of whisky. People from the other tables would turn round every now and then and look meaningfully in his direction, then turn quickly back as soon as they saw that he had noticed them.

Herne looked at the banner above the bar: *Rosie aims to please*. He wondered how successful she was – and what she used for a weapon. Maybe she would put in an appearance later in the evening and he would be able to tell for himself.

She could be an interesting woman. She certainly liked to spread her name around. It must be good for business.

As he mused, the batwing doors opened to reveal the fat shape of Joe Brodie. He scuttled half way to the bar before he noticed Herne sitting at the back of the room. He stopped dead in his tracks, gulped, turned quickly, then scuttled back out again. The doors swung back and forth behind him and all of the occupants of the saloon hollered with laughter.

Except for Herne.

Except for the figure that had appeared at the top of the stairs.

She was a little over medium height, an immediately striking woman, from the polished toes of her black boots to the uppermost wave of her flaming red hair. She was wearing a green silk dress that was cut low at the top to accentuate her already considerable cleavage. The dress was split along the left leg. The V began half way down the thigh, showing an increasing amount of tan stocking as it opened out and a bright red garter, with a yellow rose at its centre. Fractionally below the knee, stocking gave way to leather. High, lace-up boot around a well-shaped calf.

All in all, it was a truly imposing sight. Something the lady herself was fully aware of. She stood there with her left hip pushed out so as to support her angled arm – and to show more leg through the gap in her dress.

She waited motionless until she had everyone's attention. She didn't have to make a sound in order to get it. Only wait until the message was passed from one pair of lecherous eyes to the next. Then, when she was certain that all of the men had not simply seen her, but had begun to want her, she shifted her pose and started to walk slowly down the staircase.

She was watched all the way down. At the bottom, she raised both her arms towards the seated congregation. 'Good evening, boys!' she sang out.

'Evening, Rosie!' the answer poured back.

She beamed a smile, they whooped loudly. And Rosie walked the short distance to her office. Herne downed what was left of his whisky. Yes, he thought, she was one hell of a woman and she didn't care who knew it. It sure paid her to advertise and that didn't only mean the banners strung around with her name on them. He pushed his chair back on to the rear legs and swung his boots up on to the table. He didn't think she was going to reappear too quickly and he wanted to be around when she did.

Apart from wanting to get another look at her, Herne figured that if anyone knew what was going on around town she was the most likely. And he guessed that she was a sight better looking than the blacksmith.

Almost an hour later the saloon had swung into action. As much as a saloon in Charity was ever likely to muster. There were several card games in progress; there had been two minor fist fights over by the doors; some cowboy had tried to balance five full bottles of beer on top of one another and was surprised to find out that they didn't stay there. And the piano player had turned up.

That was what she had eventually turned out to be. Herne had watched bewildered as she came into the saloon. For all the world, she looked like an old-maid schoolmarm who had lost her class and didn't know where to find them.

Almost as tall as Herne himself, with a back bent from stooping forwards for most of her life and an eagle's beak of a nose, she wore a black coat over a shapeless black dress. Her hair was tied up in a bun and there was a tiny hat pinned on to it by an enormous hat pin with an enamel butterfly perched at its end.

She peered around the room rather anxiously, without anyone taking much notice of her at all. Eventually she seemed to find what she was looking for and she made her way towards it.

It was the upright piano underneath the side window.

The woman pulled a chair away from one of the nearby tables and set it in front of the instrument. Then she put her hand into the case she was carrying and pulled out a pile of sheet music which she placed in an untidy heap on the piano lid. Next she took out a pair of wire-rimmed spectacles and pushed them down over her aquiline nose. A length of black ribbon hung limply down from one frame.

One of her boney hands flipped open the music sheet at the top of the pile and she began to play. The music was fast, tinny, raggy. It fitted in with the mood and atmosphere of the saloon in a way which the player herself had totally failed.

She was half way through her second number, when the office door opened and Rosie stepped out into the main body of the saloon. She looked around for several minutes, probably assessing how much money her place had already taken that night and how much more it would pull in if she went round and jollied up the customers a little. When she had decided it was worthwhile, she moved out into the room.

It soon became clear how much difference her presence made. The laughter increased, the general level of noise almost doubled, and there was a continuous stream of people moving to and from the bar.

When things were in full swing, Rosie walked over to the bar herself. She exchanged a few words with the bartender, who handed her a bottle of whisky and a pair of glasses.

She turned and leaned her elbows back against the edge of the bar, pushing out her chest correspondingly. Both her eyes and her breasts were pointing over in Herne's direction. She hesitated, looking him over candidly, a smile playing around the curves of her lips.

Then, when she was good and ready, she swayed over to Herne's table and set down the bottle and glasses in front of him.

'Hi,' she beamed, 'I'm Rosie.'

Jed grinned back at her. 'Hell, lady,' he said, 'I thought you was Father Christmas!'

Rosie sat down beside him and slid her hand along his thigh. 'Far as you're concerned, maybe I am.'

4

Rosie's fingers spread themselves around the muscle of his leg and held it firmly. Jed did his best to ignore their presence, but it was not easy. Especially when they were no longer content to apply pressure in one spot. They were beginning to wander slowly up and down, from his knee to the edge of his groin.

He looked at her face, trying to concentrate on that instead. It was impossible to work out how old she might be – he was never very good with women's ages anyhow – but it might be anywhere between thirty and forty. For a long while she'd probably looked much the same as she did now and she would remain so a while longer.

Her face showed few lines, but the make-up she wore would have taken care of most of those in any case. Her eyes, underneath the mass of red hair, were dark brown; something about her that jarred. Almost the only thing, Herne decided.

And the hand was still moving over his thigh to the extent that he could no longer ignore it. The steadily growing swelling at the centre of his body was testament to its presence.

Rosie smiled. 'Wouldn't you like a drink, Mr Herne?'

'What's the party in honour of?' Herne asked her.

The smile broadened. 'Of you being so pleased to see me, of course.' She moved her hand deftly forwards and rubbed the backs of her nails over his crotch. 'You are pleased to see me, aren't you?'

She could damned well feel that he was!

Jed reached across for the bottle and poured two shots, passing one glass over to the hand that was on his leg so that she had to move it away to take the whisky.

Her eyebrows raised. 'What's the matter, Mr Herne? Don't you appreciate a little friendly attention?'

'Sure. But not in front of quite so many people. It makes me feel that I'm part of the hired entertainment. Like the piano player.'

'Honey,' said Rosie playfully, 'I can assure you that you are less like the piano player than anybody else I have ever seen. Or felt!'

'All right, Rosie, I take your point.'

'The question is, Mr Herne, do I get yours?'

Jed shuffled his feet awkwardly, a little taken aback by the woman's directness. It wasn't something he was used to. Saloon girls and tramps were obvious enough, certainly, but not in words.

'Since you know my last name,' said Herne, 'you must know my first. Why don't you call me Jed?'

'I will, Jed, I will. Why don't you pour me another drink?'

He looked at her glass. 'You haven't finished that one yet.'

She smiled roguishly. 'There's nothing wrong with taking two at the same time. If you've a mind to it.'

'I haven't,' Herne replied tersely.

'Fair enough.' Rosie shrugged her shoulders and downed the rest of her drink. She held the glass over towards Herne. 'Now do I get another?'

She did. And a detailed account of what had taken place outside Joe Brodie's store that afternoon. Sure, she had heard other versions but she explained that she wanted to hear the real story from the man himself. Herne assured her that it was the merest of trifles and that it would only bore her, but she seemed content to listen anyway.

'You fast with that thing?' she asked when he had finished, pointing down at his Colt.

'Fast enough. Which is all that matters. Why do you ask? Is it idle curiosity or do you have a better reason?'

Rosie pulled back her head and pouted. 'I might and I might not.'

'For a woman who was coming on mighty strong, you've gone awful bashful all of a sudden.'

She took a slug at her whisky. 'You know what we women are like, Jed, we change our moods and minds as easy as a bird flies from tree to tree.'

She pushed back her chair and stood up. 'You keep that bottle here, Jed, and carry on helping yourself. It's on the house.'

'Why's that?'

'You gave the boys something to talk about. The more they talk, the more they get thirsty. And the more my profits go up. So letting you have a drink is the least I can do.'

Jed leered up at her. 'Yes, ma'am, I do believe it is.'

She smiled openly back at him and turned to look over the saloon. Her hand was back at her hip and she was very much the actress once again. If she had ever stopped.

She watched as the doors swung open and a group of men came tumbling in loudly out of the night. One of them immediately pulled the chair out from under an unsuspecting card player and took it over to another table close to the bar. A second man took the hat off his head and, with a whoop, sent it skimming along the top of the bar, scattering full and empty glasses alike.

There were six of them all told but they managed to give the impression that they were at least twice that number. As they crowded around the end of the bar, it became clear that their leader was the wall-eyed man with a drooping black moustache and a pair of sixguns holstered for a cross draw.

It was towards this man, at the centre of the group, that Rosie walked. She kissed him on the cheek, but he grabbed hold of her and bent her backwards over the bar, pressing his mouth hard down on to hers. Herne's right hand drifted slowly from the edge of the table to his belt. The man let Rosie up and as he did so he fetched her a hefty smack across her rear.

She called out, but not in anger. Then she laughed good and loud and gave a playful tweak to one end of the man's moustache. Herne let his hand move back on to the table and poured himself another drink.

He guessed that Rosie knew what she was doing; she looked as though she could handle most men.

He hadn't been able to ask her the questions he had wanted

to, but it was beginning to look as though that would have to wait until the following day. Business in the *Queen of the West* was steadily increasing. There had to be a number of large ranches around to provide so much free-spending custom. It certainly didn't all come from the town itself. Though it was likely that people were warming themselves up for the Christmas celebrations.

Herne thought about having another drink, then decided against it. He stood up and looked around the large room. Rosie had been wandering about among her customers, but had now returned to the wall-eyed character and his friends.

Fair enough, Herne said to himself. He picked up the half-full bottle by the neck and returned it to the bar. He was on his way out when he heard his name called. It was Rosie.

She had slipped away from the rowdy group of drinkers and was walking quickly over towards Herne.

'You're not going?' she said.

'That's how it seems to me.'

'I'd thought we were going to have a nice cosy chat.'

'So had I,' said Herne, 'but that was reckoning without your friends.' He nodded past her shoulder in the direction of the cowboys she had just left.

'Aw, Jed, they're nothing. That's just business.'

'You tell that to him,' answered Herne, watching the wall-eyed man carefully.

'Don't mind him,' said Rosie.

'I don't.'

'Good.' She stepped right up to Herne and wound her arms tightly around his neck. Then she kissed him full in the mouth. The embrace was interrupted by the sound of breaking glass.

Herne swung her to one side, spanning his right hand over his Colt. At the centre of the group at the end of the bar, the man was standing in a fighter's crouch, brandishing a smashed bottle. He waved its jagged edges in Herne's direction.

'Back off! That's my woman you're messing with!'

'Who says?' Herne asked, defiantly.

The man thrust the bottle further forward. 'I say.'

'The thing is,' said Herne, 'does she?'

Rosie freed herself from Herne's left arm and stepped

between the men. She raised an arm towards each of them. 'Whoa, now, boys. We don't want anything nasty to happen here, do we?'

'That's where you're fuckin' wrong!' yelled the cowboy at the bar and made a move towards her.

'Ed!' she cried, 'you got no cause to . . . ' Rosie went up to him, left arm outstretched. The man called Ed lunged at her with the bottle before she had time to finish. Rosie screamed and jumped back. She half-turned towards Herne holding up her arm for him to see.

There was a crazed gash down the inside of it and the blood was already pouring freely from the wound. She put her other hand across to try to stem the flow, but the blood bubbled thickly through her spread fingers.

Herne looked coldly at the wall-eyed man. 'You got three seconds to drop that bottle and go for one of them guns,' he barked.

His voice was loud in the otherwise total silence of the room. Men stood on chairs, tables – anywhere to get a good view of the confrontation.

'What happens if I don't drop it?'

'Then I take you anyway.' Herne's voice was as cold as ice.

'Shit!' said the man and threw the bottle hastily in Herne's direction. At the same time his left hand clawed across in front of his chest, going for the handle of the gun that waited there.

Herne saw the broken bottle coming at his head and swivelled away to let it past. As he rocked back, all his weight thrown on to his right leg, his hand swept into a smooth circling motion and drew the Colt clear of its holster.

Hammer back, trigger back, both actions part of the same beautifully co-ordinated movement. The first shot shattered the bones at the back of the man's left wrist as the fingers dragged his gun round. Released, it fell uselessly to the saw-dust strewn floor. Before it landed, Herne's second shot had hammered into his chest immediately above the breast bone and slammed him back against the edge of the bar.

He flopped forward, down onto his knees. Arms spread wide, he stared up at Herne in the final unbelieving seconds before dying. Herne cocked back the hammer one more time and took careful aim. He shot right through the man's good eye, taking it out completely. The range was so close that a good deal of the head was blasted away as well.

One of the cowboys who had been with the now dead man looked down with disgust at the splotch of greyish matter, streaked through with red, that clung to his waistcoat.

He stared at it as though it was some strange fungus that was going to eat its way into him, then he brushed it away with his sleeve, an expression of disgust riveted to his face.

He looked at Herne over the slumped shape between them. 'What the hell did you have to do that for?' he asked hoarsely.

'What do you think I did it for?' Herne snarled. 'For one thing, he attacked this woman with a broken bottle. For another he went for his gun. Damn it! How many reasons d'you want me to have for killin' a man?'

'That depends who it is you're killin'!'

'Meaning?'

'Meaning that maybe we got plenty of reasons for taking care of you.'

Herne ran his eyes along the bar. Five men; they had spread themselves out when the wall-eyed man was making his play; now they had edged back together in the way that gangs automatically do. The one who was acting as the gang's spokesman was a swarthy, medium-built cowboy with a stetson pushed back on his head. He wore one gun peculiarly high on his hip. Unless he had some special way of using it, Herne couldn't see how he was going to be able to clear leather with any sort of speed.

The other four had nothing special to mark them out. They weren't any uglier or more handsome than any men who had spent a hard time working on the range and had come into town to loosen up and cause a little ruckus. They all wore guns – it would have been strange if they hadn't – but none seemed to be professional. They didn't have either the stance or the manner.

But they had been drinking a lot and their leader had been shot down in front of them. It was going to be difficult for them to back down and lose face in front of the town.

Yet the longer they stood there, the less likely it became that they would make any kind of move – except for the door. And all the while the blood poured from the wounds of the man crumpled on the saloon floor. Poured from his arm, his chest, from the hideous raw socket where his eye had been.

'Reckon that if I were you,' said Herne, 'I'd pick him up and shift him out of here. Before he sets in rotten and stinks the whole place out.'

Two of them pushed themselves off the bar and started to move forward, intending to do what they had been told. Two of the others were undecided, one of them the one who had been doing the talking.

Which left one other cowboy. He stood to the far right. Hadn't spoken a word nor made a move. There was nothing about him which suggested that he might do either. Until . . .

Partly covered by one of his friends who was moving between Herne and himself, he went for the gun that hung below his hip. Did more than just go for it – he drew and had the hammer cocked in a lot less time than he should have been able to manage.

Herne saw the move late and, unless he chose to shoot through the man who stood between them, had only a limited target. He loosed off a snap shot at the cowboy's gun arm shoulder. It tore away the material of the man's coat and several layers of skin, but not much more. The man's return shot went low and embedded itself high in the thigh of the friend in front of him. This set off a loud shout of pain which was repeated in kind when Herne fired his next, more measured shot. His aim was directed at the elbow and it was true.

The cowboy dropped his gun and clutched at the smashed bone of his right arm, his mouth opening with the intensity of the pain.

The scene was rapidly degenerating into an orgy of shooting and blood-letting. There were three of them remaining, one close at Herne's left side. He hadn't made a move for his weapon, but Herne was not about to take any chances. He brought the underside of his Colt round in a sweeping blow that struck the man's temple and grazed on across his forehead.

He rocked on his heels, staggered backwards and finally collapsed over the body of the wall-eyed man.

'Christ!' shouted the cowboy standing with a hand clapped desperately over the deep wound in his thigh. 'Christ almighty! Can't somebody do something about this bleeding?'

There didn't appear to be any immediate offers. No one paid any attention to his problems, least of all Herne. He was too busy trying to figure out when the two remaining desperadoes by the bar were going to make a move.

'Tell you something, mister,' said one of them.

'Make it quick,' Herne snapped.

'By my count you've only got one shell left in that gun of yours.'

'And . . . ?'

'And there's two of us.'

'All right,' said Herne, 'so which one of you wants to take the risk that it won't be him I use it on?'

The two of them looked at Herne, then at each other. Finally they got their message from the pools of blood which were settling on the floor close to their feet and from their friend with the gunshot wound in his leg who was still screaming for help.

'You're calling the shots, mister.'

'Right. Ease those guns out of your belts and slide them back along the bar. And don't be foolish. There's been enough shooting going on here for one evening.'

They did as they were ordered.

'Now get these bodies out of here – and get that feller there to a doctor. Suppose there is a doctor around here somewheres?' Herne looked around the crowd, most of whom had backed away as far as they could without losing sight of what was happening. 'Maybe one of you could fetch the doc? The rest of you could help get this mess sorted out.' He gestured down to the heap of bodies in front of him.

At first no one moved. Then a wizened old man hobbled over to the door while a few others, obviously with stronger stomachs than the rest, walked slowly and self-consciously forward from the stunned crowd to help.

Herne holstered his Colt and walked over to the bar.

'Gave you back a bottle with a whole lot of whisky still in it,' he said to the barkeep. 'I reckon I could use some of that right now.'

The bottle and a glass slid along the polished counter towards him. Herne was on his way back to his table, the one he had been sitting at before, when Rosie intercepted him. She looked a lot paler than she had and her arm had been tended to but otherwise didn't seem any the worse for what she had seen. The fact that she had triggered it all off didn't seem to be bothering her unduly. Herne reckoned that that was maybe because she was used to having men fighting for her favours.

'It's going to be difficult to talk in here for a while,' she said. 'Why don't you come into my office and have your drink?'

Herne looked coolly into her brown eyes. 'You want to *talk*?'

Shaken though she might have been, the smile she flashed up at Herne did not reveal it. Although it did suggest a whole lot! Herne walked alongside her to the office door and waited while she drew a key from the depths of her cleavage and unlocked it.

'You always keep your keys down there?' Herne asked.

'That depends what they open,' she pouted.

'You mean you got others?'

Rosie moved up to him until her body was pushing against him from the hips. 'By my reckoning, Jed, you got the key to my highway yourself.'

She stood aside and ushered him through the door in front of her.

The office was small. There was a solid looking wooden desk at its centre, with a swivel chair behind it. Alongside the window, with its blind drawn down, there was an easy chair covered in smooth tanned hide. In front of this was a smaller table.

Rosie stood behind the leather chair and motioned to Herne to sit down. 'After all that exercise, I reckon how you could use a little rest.'

Herne set the bottle and glass down on the table and settled into the comfortable leather chair. Rosie pushed the wooden swivel chair across from behind the desk and placed herself opposite him. She took hold of the bottle and poured two stiff shots. Herne grunted his thanks and swallowed the fiery whisky in one quick gulp. She looked at him surprised, then poured him another. He tossed it back the same way as the first.

A few drinks he needed; sleep he needed; he could not remember when he had last eaten and perhaps it was food that he needed most of all. As for what the lovely saloon owner was offering – it was the last thing that he either needed or desired at that moment.

'Jed,' she breathed softly.

'Yep?'

'What you did out there . . . it was wonderful.'

'Was it?' he murmured.

'Jed, you know what I mean. You were good, really good.'

Herne looked at her but did not reply.

Her hand found its way back to his knee. 'I want to thank you, Jed. Those men have been asking for trouble for a long time now. They needed bringing down like that.'

'You seemed to greet them pretty friendly,' said Herne with an edge to his voice.

She withdrew her hand and sipped at her drink. 'What else could I do? I couldn't stand up against them and there isn't anyone else in Charity who could have done it for me. All I could hope to do was to stay on their good side.'

'You sure seemed to have that operation off well.' The sarcasm in Herne's tone was even more marked.

'Jed!' Rosie's voice rose in protest. 'What are you sounding so bitter about?'

'Lady,' he said, leaning forward, 'you do realise, don't you, that had you not come and made a play for me when you did, I would have been left to walk out of there without anything happening?'

'Why, Jed, I never thought about it.'

Herne slammed his empty glass down on the low table and leaped to his feet. There was a fierce anger in his eyes that Rosie did not like. She had seen it before. And too recently for her to forget it. She had seen it when he had faced the man who had attacked her with the broken bottle. She did not like it directed towards herself. It told her all too clearly that here was a man who was dangerous; a man who spent all of his life walking on a razor's edge between life and death.

'Whatever you do, lady, don't ever make the mistake of trying to take me for a fool!' His lips were set in a snarl and his finger jabbed at her to reinforce what he was saying.

'Jed, I . . .'

He flung back his hand and she cowered back, terrified that he was going to slap her around the face. The pain from her roughly bandaged arm was already sending waves of sickness through her stomach and up to her brain.

'I'll spell it out for you the way I see it,' Herne stormed. 'You correct me if I'm wrong. Those fellers have been coming in for quite a while and getting louder and louder, more and more difficult to control. You'd tried charming 'em and that had worked for a time, but it was wearing off and you were getting frightened. You could see them running riot and wrecking your whole operation. And then I came in.

'You heard about my showdown with Brodie earlier and thought there was a chance I could get those cowboys off your back. If it went wrong and I lost out, then you weren't in any worse a position than before. If it worked then I'd get my just rewards and you'd send me on my way.'

Rosie turned away from him and faced the door.

Herne cut through the silence. 'What's the matter, lady? That getting too near to the truth for you? Admit it, you played me for a sucker. You came up and bought me for a bottle of whisky and a quick feel.'

The head of red hair sank forward a few inches. She still said nothing, nor did she move.

There was a business-like knock on the office door. 'Come in,' she said, looking up immediately.

The man who entered was silver-haired, grey-suited, a diamond tie-pin sticking from his silk cravat. He looked as though he was used to good food, good drink – and getting his own way.

He looked right past Rosie to where Herne was standing.

'Mr Herne, if you have the time there's a little business proposition I wish to put to you,' he said brusquely.

Herne had the time. He followed the man out of the room, leaving Rosie standing gaping in the doorway.

5

'Charity is a small town. Nothing more than a collection of tumble-down shacks until folks heard the railroad was coming through. That was when the bank moved in and the saloon got built. But the big boom we had all hoped for didn't happen. The railroad is used by some of the larger ranchers in the area and so the trains keep stopping. Leastways, sometimes they do.

'Groups of men from these outlying ranches drift into town from time to time. Usually after they've been paid, or to fetch supplies. Either way, they cause as much trouble as they can. Show the average cowboy something that approaches his idea of civilisation and he will do his best to destroy it. But you are a travelled man, Mr Herne. I don't need to be telling you these things.'

Jed Herne sat slightly uneasily in his chair. The banker's office was larger, more opulently furnished than the one he'd just left. The beautiful saloon owner had been replaced by a rather paunchy, smug banker. It wasn't a change that he particularly liked; though he was beginning to sense that the man's lengthy preamble might be leading up to something more worthwhile.

So he contented himself with sitting there and nodding agreement. The banker puffed away at his cigar. One of these days, Herne thought, I'll come across a banker who doesn't smoke damned cigars.

'Not being a town which receives many visitors, we tend to pay a lot of attention to those we do get. Especially those like yourself who have the appearance of being in some way – er – special.'

He put his cigar down on the edge of his desk and leaned forward with an earnest look in his eyes. 'I pride myself on being a good judge of a man's character, Mr Herne. I like to think I can sum him up in a matter of a few minutes. In my business, you have to be able to do that. It's vital to know immediately who you can trust and who you can't.'

He clamped the cigar back between his teeth, pulled hard on it, then released the thick blue-tinged smoke into the enclosed atmosphere of the room.

'I think you are a man I could trust, Mr Herne.'

Herne sensed that the banker expected him to react to this as though it was a great honour. At least as though he had just been handed a large cheque. He simply nodded rather more decisively than before. He still wanted to know what the man was leading up to.

When the banker saw that he was not going to get any verbal response, he carried on. 'Not only a man to trust, sir. More than that. I saw the way you handled that situation out in the street this afternoon. Not that I hold any brief for young Newman, none at all. But you showed an awful lot of common sense as well as a great deal of courage. It's a long time since I've seen a man with so little fear and so strong a sense of confidence in himself and his decisions.'

He exhaled more wreaths of smoke. 'Yes, sir, it was an impressive performance. Impressive. And as for what I have heard of this evening in the saloon . . . well, that beats everything. Certainly tops anything that's happened in Charity for a long, long time.'

Herne pushed himself further back into the chair and wafted a wreath of cigar smoke away with his hand. The banker seemed to puff all the more strongly.

'Would I be right to assume, Mr Herne, that you would be disposed to offer your services for a fee?'

It was the first direct question and it called forth the first direct answer.

'That's right,' Herne said.

The banker sat back with a smile on his face. An inch of

light grey ash tipped off the end of his cigar and tumbled down on to his suit.

'The job I have in mind isn't an especially difficult one, but it might require certain . . . er, skills. Skills which very few men around Charity possess.'

He stopped as he noticed Herne's expression change.

'What's the matter, sir? Did I say something wrong?'

'No. It's just that that's the third time inside a single day that someone's said something similar to me.'

'You don't mean that somebody else has already hired you out?'

'Relax. No one's done that.'

The banker looked relieved. 'I take it you're interested, then?'

'I'm interested,' Herne said. 'Depending on the job . . . and on what it pays.'

The silver-haired head came closer; the tone became more confidential. 'You'll understand that from time to time people come to owe us money; they fall behind on loan payments and such. We do our best to be sympathetic, naturally, but there comes a time when we have no alternative but to demand what is ours. It is unfortunate that our debtors are not always as reasonable as we would wish.'

'You mean,' said Herne casually, 'they object to you throwing them off their land.'

The banker sat back and bit down on the cigar. 'That, sir, is rather a harsh way of putting the situation.'

'But that's what it amounts to, isn't it?'

'Sometimes the foreclosing of mortgaged property is the only avenue left for us to take.'

'And you want me to . . . '

'The bank would like to hire you to see that its rightful business is carried out. I can assure you it will be nothing difficult for a man of your proven abilities. Merely . . . ' He freed the stump of cigar from his mouth and waved it in the smoky air. ' . . . swatting away a few flies.'

Half an hour later, Jed Herne was lying flat on his back on the hard bed he had been able to pay for with the advance the banker had given him. He stared up at the ceiling. Moonlight drifted into the room through the window, enabling him to see quite clearly.

It wasn't only the bed that made him uncomfortable. He didn't like the job he had just agreed to take on. Not that he was in any position to refuse it. He needed money to live, money for a horse and cartridges, money to get to the west coast. Until Nolan was dead he could not afford to rest. He had to take whatever work that would enable him to achieve that end.

He knew it. Knew it well. Yet . . .

He hadn't exchanged many words with young Tom Newman but he had liked him. There was an admirable open courage about the way he had faced up to the enraged storekeeper's gun. There was something about the unwavering expression in those blue eyes that marked Newman as a good man to have on your side in any kind of showdown.

And a showdown was what seemed inevitable.

For Newman and his folks had fallen six months behind with the payments on their spread. The bank had waited patiently, waited a long time, longer than most. Now they were going to foreclose. The Newmans were to be evicted the moment their final ultimatum expired.

Nine o'clock on the morning of the twenty-fifth of December . . . and they called the place Charity!

When the dawn broke on the morning of Christmas Eve, Herne was awake to greet it. He cleaned and checked his gun, pulled on his newly acquired top coat – the one he had got for helping the man he was now about to turn from his land – and walked out into the street. Rays of sunlight spread themselves over the low rooftops as Herne passed along to the livery stables to look for a good mount.

After quite a while of testing and haggling, he walked his new horse back down the street, tied it to the hitching rail, and had himself a good breakfast. It had been such a long time since he had eaten that the food was strange on the roof of his mouth.

He swung up into the saddle and took the road out of town.

The blinds above the bank's offices were still down; no need to rise early when you had others to do your bidding.

Once he had left the town behind, Herne nudged the horse into a canter. The plain spread out on either side of him, rising up high away to both right and left. There were dark clouds gathering over to the east: storm clouds. Herne pulled the collar of the thick coat up over his neck and round his ears. It was cold and getting colder.

He looked once more at the cloud formation spreading across the sky. Before the day was out, Herne thought, it would snow. The land would be covered in white. White Christmas.

He clicked through his teeth and his new mount picked up speed. The rider smiled, pleased at the animal's instant response to his instruction.

The terrain began to get rougher as Herne followed the route he had been given. He passed over a low, gradual incline and reined in. The track led down in front of him rather more steeply than it had risen. It wound to the left and passed by a small ranch building which was flanked on both sides by low barns. In front of one of these a man was busy chopping wood.

Herne watched him, recognising him as Tom Newman. He lightly touched the flanks of his horse with his spurs and jogged down the track.

He hadn't gone far, when the young man looked up. He turned quickly, dropping the axe and reaching for the rifle that was propped against a pile of logs. He raised it to his shoulder and called in the direction of the house at the same time.

Herne made no move towards his own gun, but kept moving at the same steady rate. He saw Newman lower the rifle, peer forward, then rest the butt of the weapon on the ground while he waved welcome with his free hand.

'Hi, Jed! It's sure good to see you. Didn't think you'd come out. Thought maybe you would have ridden on already. There didn't seem to be much in Charity to keep a man like you.'

He stopped talking abruptly, suddenly conscious of the fact that his voice had been high and excited and that he had been chattering away while Herne had neither spoken nor smiled.

'You all right, Jed?'

'Sure. I'm fine.'

'Good.' Tom Newman grinned up at him, clapped his hands, blew on them and then banged his arms crossways several times – over his chest.

'Hell!' he exclaimed. 'It sure is good that you rode over. The folks will be real pleased to see you. 'Specially after what I told them you did for me in town.'

'You have a funny way of welcoming visitors,' said Herne slowly, nodding down towards the rifle.

The young man followed his gaze. 'That! That weren't nothin'. Thought you might have been . . . well, someone else. Course,' he laughed, 'I recognised the coat straight off, but there's more than one of them around here.' His face clouded over. 'Doesn't do to take too many chances.'

Herne nodded.

'Get yourself down, Jed. Come in and have some coffee. Morning like this it's good to get something warm inside you.'

Herne looked across at the door to the wooden building. A man of about fifty, possibly older, stood leaning against it, a shotgun in his hand. Again, Tom followed Herne's stare. He waved an arm at the man and called out, 'It's all right, Pa, this is that Jed Herne I was tellin' you and Ma about. He's comin' in for some of that good coffee we got.'

He chuckled again and watched as his father lowered the gun and disappeared into the house. Herne dismounted and tied up his horse. Tom Newman waited and then led him inside, a friendly hand laid on his back.

He introduced Jed to his father with evident pride. Herne shook the man's gnarled hand and looked at the rheumy eyes and the white scrub of beard that was stained brown around the mouth through years of chewing tobacco. Whenever he had been able to afford it. From the face, the hand, Herne guessed that there had been many a time when he had been forced to go without.

The inside of their home was sparse and simple; it testified to a lifetime of struggle and hardship. A lifetime spent trying to succeed in building up a profitable concern so that the old man and his son could stand on their own two feet and say that what was theirs was truly theirs. So that they would not have to stand aside from other men.

And now Herne was going to help to snatch all of that away from them: their home; their land; their pride.

The coffee in his cup tasted suddenly sour.

The old man reached across with his foot and kicked at one of the logs jutting out of the fire, causing a flurry of sparks to spring forth.

'Dang me, nothin' I do seems to kindle any warmth in these old bones of mine!'

He cussed a few times, then spat down into the flames. There was a sharp hiss and crackle. The old man wiped his sleeve across his mouth.

'You aimin' on settlin' in these parts,' he asked Herne, 'or just passing through?'

'I might see out the next few days,' answered Herne. 'After that I'll be moving on.'

'Where are you headed, Jed?' asked Tom Newman.

'Down San Francisco way.'

The young man shook his head in amazement. He'd heard of the place, of course, but for all that he knew it was in another world.

'What are going all that way for?'

'Business . . . sort of,' said Herne slowly.

Tom Newman shook his head a second time. This surely was a strange man who had come into his life. He reached out a hand towards the fire and enjoyed the warmth his father could no longer feel. It was a good life really, he thought. Oh, the work was hard and they were desperate for money. There was serious illness in the family. So many things that should have gotten him down, yet . . .

He glanced at the tall, dark-haired man who sat opposite him and knew that while there were friends like him in his life he could never completely give up hope that things would improve.

Herne was staring down into the now empty mug.

'What you thinkin', Jed?'

Herne looked at the blue eyes with an expression that was

suddenly, chillingly cold. Tom drew his hand back from in front of the fire.

'What is it, Jed? What's troubling you?'

'A job I've got to do.'

'Job. What kind of job? Something that will stop you passing time with us?'

Herne nodded unhappily. 'Reckon it will, Tom,' he said heavily.

'What is this job you're all frettin' about?' asked the older Newman.

'Somethin' I have to do here.'

'Here?' Tom Newman's voice rose in surprise.

The room was abruptly quiet. The faint hissing and cracking of the wood fire seemed oddly loud and forceful.

'You can't . . . there ain't no job you could do here! It's . . . '

Tom's father interrupted him by placing his hand on his son's shoulder. 'Reckon this new-fangled friend of yorn ain't such a friend after all. He's taken sides with that bastard Mellor!'

The older man leaned forward and spat once more down into the fire.

'That's not possible!' Tom Newman pushed back his chair and stood up. The blue eyes were staring wildly down at Herne; the expression on his face one of startled disbelief. 'You couldn't have done that. Not after what you did for me yesterday!'

Herne returned his stare, saying nothing.

'Dang me, boy. Jes' see how he ain't answerin'. He's gone over to Mellor right enough.'

'Jed! Say it isn't right!' Tom Newman implored. But even as he said the words, he knew it was. A cold wave, a mixture of disappointment and fear, rolled across his stomach.

'See, Tom,' said Herne, 'what I did in Charity I would have done for anyone who seemed to be lookin' down the wrong end of a gun for no good reason at all. What I'm doin' now is a job. Paid work. I hired myself out to the only man who wanted to pay me. There's nothing personal about what I've come here for today. I'm just sorry it turned out to be you and your folks.'

'Then . . .'

'Then nothing. I may be sorry, but that won't stop me doing my job. Not now I've taken money for it and given my word.'

'Your word to Isaac Mellor!' snorted the old man. 'I'd as soon give my word to a rattlesnake! He wouldn't pay any attention to holdin' his word if it didn't suit him.'

'That don't matter none. It don't matter at all. Once I shake hands on somethin' then it's done.'

Tom Newman took a step back from him. 'You shook my hand yesterday, Jed.'

'Damn it, boy!' shouted Herne, 'that was different. You got to see that.'

Tom Newman turned away. He didn't want to see it. Didn't want to see Herne's face.

The old man spat on the boards in front of the fire. He got up slowly and ground the yellow gobbet of spittle under his foot.

Then he looked up at Herne. 'What exactly is this dang job you've come to do?'

'You got till nine in the mornin' to quit, unless you come up with the money you owe the bank. That's all.'

'All!' Tom whirled back round. 'All! What the hell does that mean? Turning a family out on Christmas Day and you say, that's all. God, Jed, yesterday I thought you was a decent man with feelings. Now I know you ain't got no more feelings than this floor.' And he stamped heavily downwards.

Herne blinked. For most of his life what the youngster had said had been right. He had felt nothing. Then Louise had opened up something in him which for years he had kept suppressed, had refused to believe existed. After that he had known what feelings were . . . but now . . .

Now it was different. Now it had to be different. Feelings were luxuries he couldn't afford.

Then he remembered Becky standing before him by the quayside in New York.

'Tom. I'll go back and tell Mellor that you'll move within the next two weeks. That will mean you and your folks can stay here for the Christmas and still have time to look around for somewhere you can move on to. How about that?'

By way of an answer, Tom Newman led Herne across the

room to a log door. He opened it, a finger to his lips, and let the tall man pass through into the room beyond.

Lying in the bed was a woman. Her hair was straggly and matted in places to her scalp. There were dark lines underneath closed eyes. A nose that was marred by scabs of purplish skin. One hand clung to the edge of the rough cotton sheet. It was as thin as the woman's hold on life.

When she breathed, her breath rattled inside her body.

Herne looked down at her, then turned quickly around and walked back into the other room.

Tom Newman closed the door behind him. 'That's my Ma.'

Herne faced him. 'Yep,' he said solemnly.

'She's wastin' away. Every day she gets thinner and thinner. We try to get her to take somethin' down, but she brings it back up again as often as not. Mostly she lies there sleeping which is a mercy. But she wakes sometimes and asks Pa or me if everything's still all right with the ranch.' He fixed his blue eyes on Jed. 'There ain't no way we're goin' to tell her that we got to move out. It ain't right. Surely you can see that, Jed? It just ain't right.'

Herne nodded. 'Mellor knows about your Ma?' he asked.

'Sure he knows. Says that's why he's given us as much time as he has. Now I suppose he can't wait any longer.'

'Seems that way.'

'This changes things, doesn't it, Jed?'

Herne looked from the youngster to his father, from his father to the door behind which his mother lay. And then he shook his head very slowly from side to side.

'What d'you mean?' Tom blurted.

'I mean it don't change a thing. It can't. Like I told you, I already took the man's money and gave him my word. If you say I can tell him you'll be out in two weeks, then I'll try and do my best for you. If not . . . then I'll be back in the morning.'

'Hellfire, son,' said the old man, 'tell this friend of yorn to get his miserable arse out of here before I fill it with shotgun pellets!'

Herne turned and saw the man with the weapon in his hands, pointing in his direction. He ignored him and looked back at Tom. 'What's it to be?'

'We ain't movin'! Not for anything. Not for anyone. Not even for you, Jed Herne.'

Herne moved towards the door. 'I'm right sorry, Tom. For you and your folks.'

He walked outside and went over towards his horse. The two men came out of the building after him, the older one with the shotgun over his crooked arm.

Herne swung himself up into the saddle. 'I'll be back at nine in the morning, Tom. For your sake, I hope you've seen sense and moved on out before I get here.'

Tom Newman stood away from his father. 'If you come here in the morning, Jed, then you'll have to come in shooting.'

Herne saw the young man's defiance in his stance, in the expression in his clear, open face. He said: 'Don't worry, son. I will.'

And he wheeled his horse around and moved on up the slope that led back to Charity. Behind him, the snow clouds still gathered, thickening with the passing of time.

6

The plain was white. A hard frost had set a crisp seal on the snow that had fallen during the night. Each forward movement the horse made cut down through the brittle crust into the softness beneath. Herne pulled hard at his coat and cursed the cold. He had jammed a stetson down on his head and bought a pair of gloves for the hands that held the reins but was still colder than he'd been for some ten years. The time he'd been trapped in a blizzard in Wyoming Territory. Then it had been more than thirty below.

Jed pulled the horse to a halt at the crest of the hill that wound down towards the Newman homestead.

He looked round behind him at the expanse of whiteness, unrelieved except for the straight line of hoof marks that marked his progress through the snow. Above him the sky was still darkly grey.

Below him . . . smoke curled up out of the chimney and was soon lost to sight. Chopped wood. A cart with a broken wheel. Away to the right of the main building a single, bare tree. All were lined with snow. Herne's attention went back to the tree. There was a flutter of movement, a flapping of wings: a large bird perched on an outflung branch, tumbling small showers of white powder downwards. Dark. Ugly. A vulture.

Not even this temperature could negate its greed; not even the extreme cold could blunt its sense of the proximity of death.

Herne wanted to draw his gun and shoot it. Instead he

moved his mount on the descent to the ranch.

He had got within fifty yards of it when a shot rang out. It was oddly muffled by the eerie, snow-filled atmosphere. Jed reined in sharply and waited. The bullet had passed well wide of him. He sensed that it had been meant as a warning. A warning that he should keep well away.

The sound of his spurs announced his decision to continue towards the building from which the shot had been fired. Another ten yards and there was a second shot. This one was closer. It dug a tunnel into the snow close to his right, causing the horse to rear up.

Herne brought him back into line and moved down once again.

This time the door of the ranch house was flung hastily open and the figure of Tom Newman jumped out. He had a rifle to his hip and even from that distance, Jed could see the anger that burned on his face.

'I warned you, Jed! I warned you what would happen!'

'And I told you that I was comin' in, no matter what you said or did.'

Newman started to lift the rifle to his shoulder.

Herne shouted down to him. 'Don't be more foolish than you need be, Tom. There ain't no point in you shootin' me, anyway. For one, you'll likely miss and then I'll have to take you myself. For two, if you did stop me, then Mellors would only send someone else. You can't win, son. Don't cause people to die when it ain't necessary.'

The young man waved the rifle in an outburst of temper. 'It's too damn late for you to talk about people not dyin'. Ma lay awake yesterday when we thought she was asleep. She heard us talking about what you'd said. When she spoke to Pa about it, what little bit of life she had left seemed to drain from her. She never said anything again. Just lay there with her mouth frozen open. All we could hear as we sat around the bed was a dry rattle at the back of her throat. 'Bout midnight she sat up in that bed as though a bolt of lightnin' had struck through her body. Arms flung out and eyes staring up above her like she'd seen something terrified her. By the time she'd fallen back on to her bed, Ma was dead.'

Herne reached up and pulled off his stetson and held it in front of him as a mark of respect.

'Tom,' he called down, 'I'm sorry. Plumb sorry. I . . . there ain't nothing more I can say.'

Tom began again to lift his rifle to his shoulder. 'You're right, Jed. There ain't nothin' more you can say. You've said enough already. What you said yesterday brought about Ma's death.'

'That ain't so, Tom. You know that. Only don't lift that gun of yours any higher. 'Cause I don't want there to be another dead body round here an' if you make a play against me I got no alternative. Not as far as I can see.'

The movement of the rifle stopped momentarily. Herne relaxed. Then another figure stepped out into the coldness of the morning. Tom's father held his shotgun in front of him, twin barrels aiming in Herne's direction, stock pulled back against his hip. He walked past his son and moved up the slope towards the spot where Jed Herne was waiting.

'You killed her! You killed her!' the old man shouted feverishly. 'My Emily. You killed her!'

His foot drove down into an especially deep patch of snow and he was stopped short. Herne looked at the old man's face; it was lined with strain and creased by year after year of hard work. Work which had proved ultimately fruitless. His eyes were flooding with tears: tears of hatred for the man sitting astride his horse on the slope above him; tears for the woman he had loved for more than thirty years. The woman who now lay on the bed that had been their marriage bed. Now the worn white sheet was pulled high over her face. And a covering of snow was over the land he had tried to tame for his own.

Old Man Newman pulled his leg high out of the deep fall and started back towards Herne. Tom Newman watched helplessly. Knowing that he should interfere; knowing also that he would get no thanks from his father if he did so.

'Mister, I'm gonna kill you if it's the last dang thing I do! My . . . my Emily . . . she was everything to me. All I ever wanted. All I . . . watching her like that . . . fading away . . . her poor body racked with pain . . . hate, that's what it is . . .

gonna make you regret that you ever come here . . . gonna . . . kill . . . kill . . . k . . . k . . .'

Saliva flew from his mouth. The man was merely babbling now, making sounds rather than words. His feet slipped and stumbled as he tried to hurry towards the man he wanted so desperately to kill. As he got nearer, Jed could see clearly where the flecks of spittle had frozen on to the ragged edges of his beard.

He looked at the man's gnarled right hand; the one close by the double trigger of the shotgun; the one which would send a devastating cascade of buckshot in Herne's direction.

'Gonna . . . gon . . . gon . . . k . . . k . . . Emily . . . kill!'

Herne looked past the man at his son, who was still waiting below with his rifle close to his shoulder.

'Tom!' Herne shouted. 'Stop him, can't you? He's gone loco!'

Tom Newman's answer flashed back, 'Don't you say that about my Pa!'

'Kill . . . kill . . . kkkk . . . !'

Herne watched as the old man lost his footing and fell forward, pushing out the gun in an effort to right himself. Half way to the ground, his fingers pressed down on the trigger.

Herne flipped himself backwards from his horse, rolling through the snow in a ball from which he emerged with his legs splayed out into a gunfighter's crouch, his Colt .45 drawn and ready.

One barrel of the old man's gun had been fired; the other was still waiting. Not for long. He looked truly crazed now. His mouth was open and hissing sounds emerged, together with a stream of spittle which dribbled down over his chin. He wasn't more than fifteen feet away from Herne and he suddenly decided that he was going to charge across that space and fire the remaining barrel full into Herne's body.

There was no way in which Jed could accept the risk – he might get close enough for it to be impossible to miss, or he might get thrown off balance the same way as a few moments earlier. In either case, there was no doubt what he had to do.

Herne fired twice. The first bullet smashed into the old man's knee cap, breaking it instantaneously into a myriad shards of brittle bone. The second almost split the wiry arm at the elbow, again rending bone and tearing through sinew.

The old man was spun round by the impact of the bullets. He balanced precariously on his left leg, staring at the shattered limbs of the right hand side of his body. A ragged scarecrow guarding a field of snow. Only not stuffed with straw. The blood that ran down into the whiteness by its feet testified to that.

Then he fell with a crunching sound as the frozen surface opened up and accepted his broken body.

Only then did Herne notice where the first charge from the shotgun had gone. It had blasted into the side and stomach of his horse. The animal lay now with its torn belly facing in Herne's direction. Coils of intestine tumbled over one another and slithered like snakes down on to the ground. Blood washed over them and soaked into the white surface, through which it spread like fire through paper.

Herne watched spellbound as the blood from the animal reached out tendrils towards that from the old man's shattered arm and leg, some five feet away.

Amazingly, the animal's head moved up off the ground and it gave an almost human whine of pain. Herne stood over it with his gun aiming downwards.

'Jed! Jed Herne!'

He had temporarily forgotten Tom Newman.

'Herne! How many more of my family you gonna kill?'

Herne ignored him and fired once through the animal's brain. Only then did he turn and face down to the ranch. Tom had shifted his ground, finding cover behind the cart to the left of the main building.

'I didn't kill your Ma and your Pa's not dead. Why the hell don't you come up here and get him into the house instead of trying to get yourself shot into the bargain?'

The answer was a bullet which ploughed into a thick drift of snow a foot or so to his right.

'The next one's going to be straighter, Jed.'

Herne had no intention of waiting to find out. He holstered his gun after snapping off a shot to keep the youngster ducked down. Then he ran hard and low, heading for the opposite end of the ranch buildings. A shot came after him, close enough for him to sense it passing by his head. He ducked lower still, tripped over something hidden under the surface of the snow and dived headlong. This time he couldn't manage an even roll, but he didn't shake himself up too badly. He pushed down on his hands and darted the final feet to the cover of the low barn.

Time to get his breath back and reload.

'Tom,' he shouted, partly stalling for the chance to prepare himself again, partly because he still hoped it would be possible not to have to shoot the youngster too. 'Tom! You hear me?'

'Sure I hear you.'

'Don't it do anything to you that your old man's lyin' bleeding up there in all that snow?'

'Sure it does. It makes me want to put a bullet from this rifle of mine right between those eyes of yours.'

'You reckon that's more important than stopping your old man bleedin' to death? Or freezin'?'

Silence. Herne guessed that the kid was thinking this last remark over. He hoped he would see sense. Something told him that he would not. Up on the tree, that was almost immediately above him now, the vulture had been joined by three others. Herne glanced at them with a growing feeling of disgust deep in his stomach.

He was surprised when Tom Newman stepped out from behind the cart. 'Jed! You put up your gun and I'll go up and get my Pa. We can sort the rest of this out later.'

Surprised and pleased.

He stood out from the side of the barn and let Tom see the Colt fall smoothly down into its holster. Tom laid his rifle on top of the cart and walked, then ran, up the slope to where his father lay.

Herne walked after him, hoping all the while that he had been right and that the old man was not dead.

Tom Newman knelt down beside the still, bent figure, putting his face close to the old man's head, anxiously searching for some sign of life. Herne saw the expression of relief flood over the boy's face, then change dramatically as he examined the damage to his father's arm and leg.

He pushed his arms underneath the old man as gently as he could, aiming to lift him up.

Herne moved forward and went down on one knee. 'Let me help you, Tom.'

The blue eyes fixed on Herne, icicle-cold.

'If you move a finger to touch him, I'll blast your damned brains out, you bastard. You were the one who did this to him, so what the hell do you want helping out now?'

Herne answered quietly, 'I don't see how I had any choice, Tom?'

'Shit! You didn't have to do what you did. He's just a harmless old man.'

Herne stood up. 'He was a harmless old man with a double-barrelled shotgun in his hand and a mind to use it. That's how harmless he was.'

Tom Newman raised his father's body up slowly and looked again at Herne. 'You still didn't have to do this to him. You didn't have to shoot him where you did.'

'I aimed to stop him running and stop him firing.'

'I reckon as how you did a sight more than that!'

Tom Newman turned away and walked down to the homestead, his father cradled in his arms. Herne waited a while then followed after him, watching the drip, drip of blood that fell from the old man's body.

Two hours later, the sky outside had darkened. Within the small ranch house, things were darker too.

Herne had paced around the room, watching while Tom Newman washed and dressed his father's wounds as best as he could in the poor light. He had made one further offer of help, but this had been refused with such ferocity that Herne had not thought to make another.

The old man had come round in the middle of his son's attentions.

The mixture of pain and understanding of what had happened to him had unloosed a sobbing, choking stream of cusses and moans. Finally, he had lapsed into semi-consciousness.

Tom Newman spoke. He did not look at Herne, but there was no one else in the room that he could have been speaking to. 'If he lives through this, then he's going to wish he hadn't. What use is an old man with only one good leg and one arm? What damn use is he? 'Specially without a place to live.'

Then Tom turned and set to work on his other task. He fetched a shovel and walked around to the back of the buildings.

He dug downwards, pushing with all of his strength. The ground was frozen solid beneath the soft snow covering. It was going to be a hard, difficult task. Tom kept digging till the exertion of his efforts brought sweat to his forehead and tears to his eyes. He stopped and leaned forward over the handle of the shovel, breathing unevenly. He was exhausted.

He looked up and saw Jed Herne standing opposite him holding a spade he had fetched from the barn. Tom wanted to shout, to tell him to go away, to leave him alone with the job of burying his mother. He didn't even have the strength left to do that.

So Herne began to dig, slowly lifting and turning back the clods of dark earth. Tom Newman joined him after a while. The two men worked on in a strange atmosphere of extreme cold and extreme heat. There were times when their sweat turned to frozen beads on their faces.

Eventually the grave was ready, a six-foot deep hole of cold, forbidding earth.

Tom went into the house and lifted back the sheet that masked his mother's body. He picked her up as easily as if she had been a child's plaything and carried her outside. He laid her down in the snow. Jed walked back into the house and returned a moment later with a blanket. He offered it to the kneeling youngster.

'It's better,' he said softly.

Tom Newman stood up, accepted the blanket, then bent forwards and wrapped his mother's body inside it. He lifted the bundle up and took it over to the grave. He lowered it slowly into the hole in the ground then picked himself up off his knees and stood for several silent minutes looking down on the huddled shape.

New flakes of snow began to fall on the dark material of the blanket.

Tom picked up one of the shovels and started to throw the earth back down into the hole. Herne decided that it was better if he didn't help him. Not now.

As he stood watching, something caused him to turn his head. At the corner of the ranch buildings was the figure of the father, leaning unsteadily against the wooden wall, observing the burial of his wife by his son.

And all around them and over them the snow tumbled down in ever-thickening sheets.

And it was Christmas Day.

Jed Herne stood in the doorway, watching as Tom Newman put another couple of logs on the fire. Now was the time.

'What's it goin' to be, Tom?' he said quietly, an edge to his voice.

The young man turned slowly, conscious of the fact that the big man he had sought to take for a friend had made his decision. Behind him, hungry flames licked around the new wood, seeking to consume.

'There's only one way it can be, Jed. I ain't goin' to move from here. Not now. Not ever. Unless you make me.'

'That's what I bin paid to do, son.'

'I know it.'

Neither man spoke for several moments. They could hear the uneasy breathing of the old man in the next room.

'Where's it to be,' asked Herne, 'in here?'

Tom shook his head. Herne turned and stepped outside into the open. The snow was still falling but that hadn't deterred the vultures, who were swarming around the open belly of the horse that lay on the hill. They pushed at one another with their wings, jostling for space, hopping the length of the carcass in an ungainly way, beaks wrenching at the exposed entrails and still-warm flesh. Eager to take what they could before it froze into a solid mass.

Herne ignored them; walked away to his right; waited to see what the youngster would do. The least he could do was allow Tom to call things his way.

Unless . . . 'Tom. Why don't you let me help you shift out of here, I . . .'

'No! My ma died here and I reckon my pa's goin' to. This place is all we got. All *they* ever had. All I ever had. I reckon it's a good enough place for me to go in, if that's what's meant to happen.'

Herne nodded stiffly. 'You said your piece, Tom. Now make your play.'

The young man held his rifle across his body, level with his waist. Herne guessed he would either try to bring it up to his shoulder or chance a snap shot from the hip. Jed pulled off his right glove and flexed his fingers slowly, worried about the intense cold that was already spreading through them. Hoping it would not be too long before the affair was over.

A large snowflake broke damply above his left cheek. He instinctively raised his gloved hand to brush it away, at which moment Tom Newman chose to go into action.

He swung the rifle towards Herne and squeezed off a shot. And missed. The youngster fired again, stabbing clumsily at the trigger in his haste. And missed again. Herne stood his ground.

Tom lifted the rifle up towards his shoulder.

As he did so Herne shouted out his name. Tom hesitated, just fractionally, then continued to level the sights in front of one of his clear blue eyes.

Herne drew smoothly, effortlessly. He was not going to make a mistake. He took aim at a point above Tom's rifle and fired.

The youngster's body jerked backwards, both feet momentarily raised from the ground. The rifle was thrown upwards, spinning uselessly away. At the centre of his clean, unlined forehead a crimson star had burst forth, the only bright thing in the entire landscape. The body lay completely still. Tom Newman was dead. The snow was still cascading down, quickly covering the corpse in a fine white powder.

Herne holstered his Colt, pulled his glove from out of his belt and slipped it back on his hand. Then he walked into the house and went over to where the old man lay on his bed.

He was awake with his head turned towards the door. His watery eyes showed no surprise at seeing Herne. It was almost as though he was expecting him.

The voice was so weak that Herne had to bend low over the

bed to hear what the old man was saying. 'You killed him, didn't you?'

'Yes,' Herne said, then stood up straight.

The old man seemed to nod to himself, then his eyes closed.

Herne bent forward again. 'When I ride back into town I'll get someone to come out and see to you. Look after you; move you into Charity. You just hang on here while I'm gone.'

The man's hand pushed up out of the covers, the swollen knuckles bulging prominently. The fingers pointed past Herne towards the pistol that rested on the shelf above the fire.

Herne followed the gesture, got up and fetched the gun over to the bed. He checked that it was loaded and laid it alongside the old man's head.

'That'll keep you safe enough till someone gets out here. The doc will have you patched up and right in no time.'

He moved away and slipped quietly out of the door. Outside the snow seemed to be easing, but the sky was still dark and the clouds were low over the horizon.

Herne looked across at Tom's body, lying upturned on the ground. Two vultures were sitting astride either shoulder, pecking down at his eyes. Herne rushed at them, waving his stetson. They fluttered with a noisy beating of strong wings upwards to their perch on the tree.

Tom Newman's face stared vacantly up at him from eyeless sockets, blood coursing down his cheeks.

Herne quickly saddled one of the ranch horses and rode away up the slope, past the ravaged guts of the animal he had come in on, to the top of the hill overlooking the Newman homestead.

He looked back down. The vultures were gathering once more around Tom Newman's corpse. A single shot rang out from inside the ranch house.

The birds rose upwards, flapping heavily into the leaden grey sky. Harbingers of death celebrating a feast day. Herne turned his horse's head and rode slowly away across the crisp white expanse of land that seemed to stretch forever.

7

Two days had passed. Jed Herne had been busy. Swatting more flies. News of what had happened out at the Newman place had spread like wildfire. He didn't have any more trouble collecting back payments or moving folk off property that was no longer theirs. Nobody else was as brave as the Newmans – or as stupid.

In Charity itself, people walked over to the other side of the street to avoid him. He still sat alone at his table in the saloon, but now nobody talked about him openly.

Rosie had made it clear that as long as he used her place he could expect to get served; but nothing more.

None of this upset Herne in the least. He was used to it.

Well, thought Herne, now my job's done here. And tomorrow I can make my way west.

He climbed down from his horse and tied it to the hitching post outside the bank. He walked in through the doors and went over to the teller, a nervous-looking man with a green eye-shade and a stammer whenever he was agitated. He was agitated right now. It took him several minutes to ask Herne what he wanted and several more minutes to explain that Mr Mellor was out of the bank. He had taken a good customer over to *The Queen of the West* for a drink.

Herne nodded and strode out. He'd finished his work. He had no intention of waiting to be paid for it.

Mellor was sitting close to the piano, talking earnestly to a cattle buyer who was wearing a long button-through coat which had once been white. Herne went over and stood a couple of feet back from their table.

The banker looked up apprehensively. 'What is it, Herne?'

'I finished.'

'Well, that's dandy. My congratulations on doing such a fine job in such little time.'

'It ain't your thanks I want,' said Herne sharply, 'it's my money.'

'Won't that wait until I've finished?' flustered Mellors.

'No,' replied Herne. 'It won't.'

'But I'm conducting my business and . . . '

'And nothing. You been havin' me throw folks off their land 'cause they didn't pay you in time. Our agreement was that you paid me when I'd done. Well, I've done and here I am.'

The cattle buyer had been watching Herne closely. Now he spoke. 'Your name's Herne. Does that make you the feller they call Herne the Hunter?'

Herne nodded. 'Some folks tag me that.'

'Heard a lot about you. Been hearing it for years now. Wasn't sure you were around any more. Specially not round these parts.'

'I shan't be for long,' Herne told him. 'Soon as I get my money and I've got my supplies, I'll be moving out.'

The cattle man stood up and offered Herne his hand. 'I'm proud to meet a man with your reputation.'

Herne shook the offered hand.

'And now,' continued the man in the long coat, 'I'll be content to wait a while. I guess Mellor will be going over to his bank to pay you your dues.'

The banker stood up, a scowl on his face, and brushed past Herne on his way to the door.

Ten minutes later, Herne was marching into Joe Brodie's general store. The short, fat owner backed away along the counter. The gunfighter's presence obviously disturbed him.

'Get back here, Brodie!' ordered Herne. 'I ain't about to hurt you. Not unless you try short changin' me. I need a whole mess of things. Got a journey to make. A long one.'

Joe Brodie moved back to serve him with a smile playing around his lips. Anything that he could do which would get the man out of Charity he would do with pleasure, even as far as throwing in a few things at a special discount.

'You quittin' today?' Brodie asked as he busied himself with Herne's order.

'Sunup tomorrow most likely,' Herne told him. 'I'm not going to get far enough with what's left of daylight for it to be worth moving sooner. Sorry to disappoint you, Brodie.'

'No, no, sir. No, sir, I didn't mean that at all. Not at all.' His fingers fumbled with the boxes of cartridges and a number of shells bounced down on to the floor. Brodie climbed down and scrabbled about, picking them up.

'Damn me, Brodie! You were making like a pretty big man the first time I ever saw you. What's made you so all-fired nervous?'

'Nothing, sir. Nothing at all.'

'Get a move on then!'

The storekeeper did as he was commanded and when most of the things were tied and ready, Herne reached down one of the rifles from the wall behind the counter. A single shot .55 Sharps.

It didn't have the fast repeating action of some of its rivals, but it was more accurate over a greater distance. Besides, Herne was a man who only usually needed one shot.

He paid for his purchases and carried them back to the hotel. His intention was to make the journey to San Francisco partly by train, partly on horseback. He had bought a good mount which would travel with him, using one of the box cars.

Herne looked at the sky anxiously. It would soon be dark. Good. That meant it would be light again all the more quickly. He could hardly wait to be away.

Since Christmas Day the weather had held fast. It was getting warmer and there hadn't been any more snow. He hoped he would have a good ride across Kansas.

But that was tomorrow – what of tonight?

Always a man of action, Herne hated those times when he was forced to wait to make the next move. He left the small hotel and wandered down to the saloon.

The usual crowd of men were sitting around and they hushed their voices and looked away almost as soon as Herne entered. He ordered a whisky and stayed by the bar to drink it. As he leaned forward, eyes carefully checking each new customer through the long mirror as they came in, he began to wonder how long it would be before Rosie made her entrance.

With that in mind he called the bartender over and asked for a bottle. He took the familiar bottle and glass over to what had become, even in that short space of time, his usual table. No one else had used it since that first night he had sat there.

Herne stayed seated and drank steadily. He could hold his liquor better than most. It didn't seem to dull his reflexes or make him boisterous. The only effect drinking had on him was to make him somewhat maudlin, bringing back memories of a past which could never be recaptured.

Night set in and more customers came with it. But there was no Rosie at the head of the stairs. No Rosie looking down upon her faithful and preparing to make her descent amongst them.

Herne sighed, sank down the whisky that was in the glass, took the rest of the bottle back to the bar, settled his account and pushed his way out through the batwing doors, back to his hotel.

Outside his room something made him stop. He didn't know what. Just a prickling sensation at the back of his neck that made him momentarily uneasy. He listened, but could hear nothing. He tested the door of his room; it was still locked.

Shaking his head, putting the experience down to the whisky he had drunk, Herne took out his key and unlocked the door. He pushed it open and stepped inside. The interior was dark. He could only just make out the shadowy shape sitting in the chair.

His gun was in his hand in a split second. The shape made no attempt to move.

'Who the hell is it?'

There was silence.

Herne eased back the hammer of his Colt with his thumb. In the stillness of the room the action sounded remarkably loud.

'I'm givin' you three seconds to say who you are and what you're doin' here. Then I'm going to shoot.'

The shape in the chair stirred. 'Now, Jed, that isn't the warmest welcome I've been given.'

Herne holstered the gun as swiftly as he had drawn it, then moved across to the lamp. He struck a match against the heel of his boot and turned up the wick. The oil caught fire and an orange glow spread round the room.

He looked at Rosie as she sat in the chair. Her red hair shone in the light. She was wearing the same green gown that she had worn that first evening. She looked even more attractive, inviting, than she had then.

'How did you get in here? The room was locked.'

Rosie shrugged an elegant shoulder. 'Who can say? Maybe I smiled at the clerk by the desk. Does it matter?'

'It just might.'

'Why's that, Jed?'

'It depends why you've come.'

By way of an answer, she got up slowly and walked the short distance between them. She slid her arms around his neck and pushed her face up to his. Herne lowered his mouth on to hers and kissed her. She was warm and yielding; the soft flesh of her pouting lips moved over him like velvet.

When they finally broke apart, Herne said, 'I thought you'd changed your mind about me.'

'What do you mean?'

'I thought you'd used me for what you wanted, then when you heard about what happened at the Newman place you'd turned against me like everyone else. Not that I'd blame you for that. I didn't like what I did either.'

Rosie pushed herself against him. 'Jed, I'll be honest with you. I didn't think any the worse of you for what happened out there. I was sure there were reasons, things you didn't bother to explain because you figured it wasn't anybody else's business. But most folks thought you were wrong and I couldn't risk losing custom by showing what I felt for you in front of everyone. I've got to survive here after you've gone, Jed Herne. And by morning you'll only be a memory and a good yarn to tell in exchange for a beer or two.'

Herne raised his fingers to the back of her neck and stroked it gently underneath her hair. He had not acknowledged to himself that he had wanted her there, but now that she was standing pressed against him, he knew it to be so.

It had been a long time since he had had a woman – any woman. And a woman like Rosie . . .

'I'll say one thing for you,' he said, 'you're not afraid of being honest. With me anyway.'

She kissed him again. 'That's easy with you, Jed. I know you'll soon be gone and it won't matter. Nothing I say or do will matter. We'll never see each other again.'

Herne moved her backwards in the direction of the bed. They lay down alongside each other and he ran his hands along the smooth material of her dress, the shiny surface of her leather boots.

'You see, Jed,' she said softly into his ear, 'it isn't every day a man like you comes to Charity . . . and a woman has to make the most of her opportunities in these parts.'

Herne grinned. 'Which parts are those?'

Rosie pushed her tongue deep inside his ear and reached both hands downwards.

Herne was dressed and ready to leave when he realised that she was awake. She rubbed her eyes and pushed back the hair that had tumbled across her face.

'You were going without saying goodbye weren't you?'

'Yep. Reckoned we said that a-plenty last night.'

Rosie smiled. 'You're right. We did.' She pulled the covers back over her naked body and curled up.

Herne opened the door. Suddenly she sat up. 'Jed?'

'Yes.'

'One thing I want to ask you. Who's Louise?'

Herne stepped out into the passageway and shut the door firmly behind him.

Pardoe was still staring, fascinated, at the bartender. He couldn't believe such devotion to one's own nose.

Herne called over his shoulder, 'What does a man have to do to get a drink around here?'

There wasn't any answer.

Pardoe looked straight at the man. 'You aren't deaf, friend, I trust? You heard what my companion asked?'

Still the man said nothing. The bulging nostril moved with the pressure of the finger scraping around inside it.

Suddenly Herne whipped round, his gun gripped firmly in his hand. 'See this?' he demanded, thrusting the end of the barrel close to the barman's head. 'Well, if you don't get your goddamn finger out of there right now and serve us, I aim to jam this gun right up that nose you're so fond of. And if you want it cleaned out, well, I'll do a good job of that by squeezing the trigger.' He pushed the Colt even further forward, so that its tip was against the end of the man's nose. 'You got that?'

The barkeeper got it. He removed his finger, wiped it slowly but carefully over the front of his grubby shirt, then shifted a couple of paces along the bar.

'What'll it be, gents?'

Pardoe heaved a sigh of relief. 'A whisky for my friend and a brandy for myself.'

'Sorry, gents. Can't do that.'

'What the hell do you mean, you can't do that?' stormed Herne angrily.

'Just can't.'

'Why not?' asked Pardoe.

'We ain't got no whisky and we ain't got no brandy.'

'This is a saloon, I suppose?' enquired the gambler sarcastically.

'Sure is.'

'Then you do serve liquor?'

'Sure do.'

'But not whisky or brandy?'

'Nope.'

'May I be so bold as to enquire what you do serve?'

'Beer.'

'That's all?' asked Pardoe in amazement.

'Yep. Only got beer.'

The gambler looked away in disgust. Herne ordered two beers. Having waited so long, he didn't want to walk out again without having got some satisfaction.

They took the glasses of frothy liquid over to an empty table. The bartender went back to his favourite pursuit of picking his nose.

'How many saloons you been in in your whole life?' Herne asked when they were sitting down.

Pardoe shrugged his handsome shoulders.

'Hundreds, likely?' Herne persisted.

'That would be a reasonable approximation.'

'All right. Tell me this. You ever been in one as miserable as this one?'

Pardoe laughed and sipped at the beer. He made a face. 'Good God. Even this stuff tastes foul!' He set the glass down quickly and returned to Herne's question. 'Not many as bad as this. Though there have been times when I've been down on my luck and I've spent evenings in cantinas where you could have scraped the vomit off the floor with a knife.'

Herne nodded behind them. 'You'd better tell our friend down there. It sounds the sort of place he'd really feel at home in.'

The two men laughed so loudly that the other people in the bar turned their heads round to see what was happening. They weren't used to the sounds of laughter in that dismal place.

When both of them had calmed down, Herne said more seriously, 'Tell me to mind my own business if you like, but when I called your name back there in the booking office, there was something not right about the way you reacted. As though you were expecting trouble. That so?'

Wayne Pardoe stretched out his legs under the table and pushed his body back in the chair. 'Well, you noticed correctly. It isn't worth keeping a secret, so I'll tell you what happened. Between Kansas City and Denver, I got to playing a little poker. More than a little, actually, we kept going near enough all the way. Didn't even bother to sleep as far as I can recall. Players came and went along with their luck, but there was a constant group that kept going all the while.

'Two of these started out really well. Father and son. Reckoned they'd sold a ranch and were heading out westwards to buy a larger one. They had a lot of money, anyway. Like I said, at first they added to the pile they'd already got. It wasn't till we were getting nearer to Denver that things began to change. I put it down to tiredness on their part. Their concentration went and luck went riding off with it.

'By the time we were pulling into Denver they were holding a lot less than they'd started with. Anxious not to stop there, they asked for a continuation in the town. I agreed. Couldn't think of a good reason for not doing so.' He paused and looked over at Herne. 'That might have been a mistake.'

'You lost?' Herne asked.

'My good friend, if I had lost then there would not have been a problem. I won.'

'And that was bad?'

Pardoe nodded and smiled grimly. He picked up his glass of beer but before he set it to his lips he remembered what it tasted like. He put it down again hastily.

'I am afraid to say that I cleaned them out. Both of them. Every last cent they had.'

'I don't imagine,' said Herne, talking slowly, 'that they took much to that.'

The handsome head moved from side to side. 'No sir, they did not.'

'And now they're aimin' to get their money back.'

'I suspect that to be the case. You see, Jed, it is unfortunate that I do have a tendency to win a whole lot more than I lose. Now as far as I am concerned that is fine, but others don't see it that way.'

'Like those who are doin' the losing.'

'Especially those who are doing the losing.'

'And these two, they're coming after you?'

Pardoe said, 'According to what I heard. I didn't stay around to find out if it was true. One man I can handle, but two is stacking the odds too heavily against me. Both of them looked as though they would know one end of a gun from the other.'

Herne shook his head. 'Funny it should be a father and son.'

'Why's that?'

'Back there in Charity. Met up with another pair like that.'

'What happened to them?' Pardoe asked.

Herne looked at him. 'Guess they weren't lucky either.'

The platform which ran alongside the rail track at Ogden was far more substantial than the one back in Charity. So was the town it served. So were the people who used it.

Herne and Pardoe stood in the midst of a sizeable crowd of waiting men and women. Some of them were there for the same reason as themselves – to get on the train west. Others were there to meet folk who were due to arrive. Most of them were dressed up in their best clothes and whereas Pardoe fitted in well, Herne was feeling a little out of place. He was wearing basically the same things as he'd left New York in. Baths hadn't exactly been a regular feature of his journey. Now, when he lifted his arms, the smell of his own sweat was no longer the friendly, welcoming smell that a man's sweat should be. Even Herne winced as the odour assailed his nostrils.

He took good care to stand to the windward side of the smartly dressed gambler.

It wasn't too long before the train came into sight from the east, steam rising high into a dull January sky. It would stop long enough to take on water and a new crew, then leave with a lot more passengers and baggage.

Herne looked along the carriages of the train as it pulled in, seeing the faces of people anxiously looking for those who were supposed to be meeting them. Pardoe's eyes were claimed by a beautiful young woman who could not have been more than eighteen. She was wearing a smart green suit and a neat little hat with a half-veil. She rubbed her slender hands together inside kid gloves as she waited for the train to pull to a halt.

The gambler wondered if the man she was so evidently waiting for was worth it. He looked again at her face and felt a twinge of jealousy run through him. It was one of the problems of the life he led which kept him permanently on the move. He supposed that Jed Herne's life followed much the same pattern. He wondered if he had ever been able to find a woman of his own and settle down. He determined to ask him whenever the next opportunity arose.

But now Herne was grasping his arm and talking quietly and quickly. 'That pair you mentioned might come lookin' for you. Was the father a tallish feller with jet black hair and a stubbly face? The son a few inches shorter, but with the same dark hair? A suggestion of a limp?'

Pardoe gasped in astonishment. A worried frown crossed his brow.

'Heavens, Jed! You got the both of them off exactly. How did you know?'

'I knew because a couple like that just this minute got off the train.'

The gambler followed Herne's pointing finger. Although his view was partly obscured, there was no mistaking the two men as being those who had sworn to get their own back on him. Even if it meant taking their money from his body after he was dead.

Herne saw to his surprise that the gambler had already freed the derringer from beneath his coat sleeve.

'You're not aimin' to use that toy here, with all these people milling around?'

'Not unless I have to. But I certainly aim to be prepared and ready.'

Herne pushed him in the direction of the train. 'You get on board as fast as you can and hope they don't notice you in the crowd.'

'Where are you going?'

'I've got a horse that's supposed to be being put on the train at the far end. I want to make sure about that. You take my advice and do as I say.'

The two men separated. Herne pushed his way through embracing families and would-be travellers who were clamouring around the steps at the ends of the carriages.

The platform was a hubbub of voices – but not loud enough to cover the shout that rose up from the centre of the platform.

'It's him! There he is. The lowdown cheatin' bastard!'

Herne swung round swiftly. In front of him everything seemed frozen into a still tableau. Greeting and parting were halted in mid-kiss or mid-sentence. Several heads swivelled in the direction of the person who had called out. They saw a broad-shouldered, dark-haired man standing a few feet in front of a rather smaller, slightly mirror-image of himself. Both men were wearing short wool coats; both were evidently armed. The one who had shouted was pointing in the direction of the train.

On the steps, halfway between the wooden planks of the platform and the shelter of the train, was the neatly attired figure of Wayne Pardoe. The bright white lace of his cuffs and shirt front shining out like beacons.

Then all was pandemonium.

The older of the two men drew his gun and fired at the gambler. It was a hasty shot and a long way off target.

That made no difference.

Women began to scream and shout out, joined by the angry voices of men. Everyone was pushing everyone else, trying to move without knowing where they wanted to go. All they did know was that they had to get away. Fast.

The entrance to the ticket office was jammed. People tried to find alternative ways of leaving the station. Cases were knocked over or tripped over. More shots rang through the tumult. It wasn't easy to see who was firing at whom, but Herne guessed that the two ranchers were busy taking pot shots at the side of the train. Pardoe seemed to have jumped on board.

The two men continued to fire, although it didn't seem possible that they could hope to hit the gambler they were out to get.

A woman's voice screeched out in sudden and violent pain.

For a couple of seconds, all movement halted once more.

Herne saw a young woman sink to her knees, clutching at her breast. She looked deathly pale, an expression of total horror on her lovely face. Her head drooped forward, the dark veil of her dainty hat falling over her tear-scarred eyes.

There was movement again. Only now it was even more urgent. Individual voices rose up out of the general mêlée, one across the other:

'That poor girl's been shot . . .'

'Some crazy bastard with a gun . . .'
'Couldn't someone get a doctor . . . ?'
'I only came here to meet a friend . . .'
'Is somebody trying to hold up the train . . . ?'
'Why doesn't someone do something . . . ?'
'Isn't there a sheriff somewhere . . . ?'
'My God, she's bleeding like a stuck pig . . .'
'Can't somebody get the man who done it . . . ?'

Herne heard them all. Listened. Watched. Waited. The man who had almost certainly shot the girl by mistake was barging his way through the crowd of people who were still massed on the platform. His gun was gripped firmly in his right hand and he wore an expression of grim determination on his face. His son, also armed, was pushing along after him, dragging his bad leg behind him.

Of Pardoe there was still no sign. Herne wondered if he was keeping out of sight on the train, or whether he had jumped off on the other side and got away altogether?

The question was soon to be answered.

As the older man climbed up on to the train, a laced cuff emerged through one of the windows, fingers wrapped tight around a small gun. There was a shot like a whipcrack and the swarthy man looked round, shaken but not hit. He was awkwardly placed for using his own gun, to get a good shot at the gambler. Not so his son. He was standing with clear space all around him and his weapon was already raised to take aim on the gambler.

His shooting wasn't as good as his situation. The bullet smashed into the window at a spot above where Pardoe had been a couple of seconds before.

And then Pardoe appeared at the other end of the carriage; the end nearest to Herne himself.

'Look! There he is!' The shout turned the heads of all those still on the platform. It also allowed the son a second chance. This time he was more fortunate: perhaps Wayne Pardoe's luck was on the turn.

The slug entered the upper part of the gambler's right arm, causing the pearl-handled derringer to clatter down on to the wooden boards.

A large space cleared around the men. Father and son, the one resting his gun arm on the rail of the train steps, the other grinning from ear to ear.

'I got him, pa! I got him!' he cried out excitedly.

'You did well, boy. But there's more to be done yet.'

'Like gunning down a few more innocent women?' asked Pardoe calmly. He sounded as if nothing untoward had happened, though it was evident from the blood which had already begun to stain the previously white shirt cuff, that he was in considerable pain.

'Don't start blaming me for that,' shouted the man on the steps. 'How d'you know that wasn't your work? Seems the sort of low-down thing you would do.'

'Sorry to disoblige you, gentlemen,' said Pardoe, 'but I am not in the habit of shooting young women. Especially beautiful ones. Besides, a comparison of the bullet hole with my own gun and yours will soon show the truth of what happened.'

The son interrupted. 'Don't let him babble on, pa. He's just stallin' for time. Let's finish him now.'

Of course, Herne realised, the young man with the limp was right. It was exactly what the gambler was doing. It was a gambler's way out of the situation. The only way out. Keep a straight face and stay calm – on the surface.

Even if there were a gunshot wound in your arm that was causing you merry hell and your weapon was down on the floor way out of reach. Even if you were staring at two guns that were aiming right at you. You still didn't panic.

It was like knowing that you were sitting facing a man holding all four aces. You just hung on in there and waited for a lucky break.

Herne wondered where the gambler was going to get his joker from this time. Unless he had another of those tricky little weapons stashed away somewhere, he couldn't see how he was going to get out of this one.

A gambler trapped without an ace in the hole.

Unless . . .

Unless Jed Herne was just that ace.

He didn't know. It wasn't his fight. Pardoe wasn't even specially a friend. Besides which, he'd already helped him out once. He didn't feel like making a habit of it. The last time, all he'd needed to do was draw his Colt and show it around. If he butted in on this one, he would have to do more. A whole lot more. Like face up to a couple of ready drawn guns and likely get to kill another man or two.

But he was fairly certain that Wayne Pardoe wasn't a cheat and that he'd won the money off these men fairly. Not only that, there was a young girl bleeding to death further up the platform and nobody paying a blind bit of attention to her. Almost certainly, her death would be due to the big rancher's thoughtless haste to get his own back on the man who'd outsmarted him.

'Come on, pa! Let's finish him and get our money back.'

'Don't worry, boy. He isn't about to go anywhere. In fact you could say that his ticket for this train was nothing more nor less than a waste of money.'

Herne watched as two sets of eyes narrowed. He glanced quickly at Pardoe, anxious to see if he was about to make a second move.

But there was no move for the man to make.

Herne had figured that while the son was probably the faster shot, the father was likely to be the straighter. Which meant going for the slower man first. He'd have to let Pardoe figure out a way of taking care of the son.

He was glad that it wasn't his own life he was gambling with. But then, he doubted if he would have allowed himself to get into the situation where was staring down the barrels of two men's guns without a weapon of his own.

'Pa!' shouted the son excitedly.

'You're plumb right, boy. Let's finish him.'

Herne went for his Colt fast, firing the first shot from the hip. He saw the big man wheel round on the steps clutching his left arm, dropping his gun as he did so. The other man had taken one shot at Pardoe, but, fortunately for the gambler, his anxiety to get rid of him had got the better of his aim. He didn't get the chance to try again.

Herne fired once more, catching the younger man between the right shoulder and the chest. Another weapon fell to the platform and slithered over the boards.

Wayne Pardoe hurried forward and seized the nearest gun.

'Thanks once again,' he shouted back over his shoulder to Jed. 'It seems I am to be permanently in your debt.'

'That's okay,' returned Herne. 'Maybe some day I'll find a way of letting you repay me.'

'What shall we do with these two?' Pardoe asked, gesturing with the gun at the wounded men.

'I don't know,' said Herne. 'I thought you'd have a few ideas about that.'

'I have several ideas that I'd be only too happy to try out,' admitted the gambler, 'only I don't think they're particularly legal.'

'Maybe that's for me to decide.'

All four men looked over towards the side of the platform. The man who had spoken wasn't much older than twenty-two or three. He had a neat brown moustache above his lip and high on his right cheekbone there was a round purple birth mark. He was wearing a black waistcoat, black shirt and black pants. In his hands there was a Remington 10 gauge shotgun with 28 inch double barrels. A belt that went diagonally across his chest held a Remington Frontier .44. At his hip, as if to prove that he wasn't overly partisan in his choice of weapons, there was a Colt Peacemaker .45, complete with mother-of-pearl grip on which was depicted an eagle with a snake in its mouth.

On the opposite side of his chest to the Remington pistol was a marshal's star.

Hell, thought Herne, he sure isn't about to take any chances.

The marshal jerked the shotgun in Herne's direction. 'Nice and easy, now. You slide that Colt of yours back into its holster. That's the way. Now you . . . ' He moved the gun round to Pardoe. ' . . . drop that thing back where it was a moment ago, before you fellers started shooting one another up.'

The wounded rancher on the steps interrupted him. 'You mean you were here then and you let all this happen? You let that man gun me through the arm that way?'

The marshal smiled, his moustache lifting higher at one side of his mouth than the other. 'Never reckon to stop folks I don't know killing themselves. Usually find they needed to die anyway and it saves me a lot of trouble. Not to mention shells. See, the town pays for the cartridges I use. They appreciate it if I let others do the shooting for me.'

'But that man opened up on us for no reason. Our quarrel wasn't with him.'

The marshal moved the shotgun round towards the rancher on the train steps. 'Seemed to me that you were about to let fly at a man who didn't have a gun on him at all. That was all right by your reckoning, I suppose?'

'That was different. He cheated us out of our money.'

The marshal shrugged. 'That's as may be. I don't see how it gives you the right to start a fight with guns here on the station with so many folk around. Looks like that young lady there might be dead already. That being so, you're going to be hanging around here for longer than you might have expected.' He chuckled boyishly. 'We have our own way with killers round here. We take them out to a big old oak on the edge of town and organise a grand picnic. Town band gets to play, kids have their games and all – then as a sort of climax to the whole affair, why, we throw some rope over that old oak and watch you swing. Then everyone collects up their picnic things and goes home.'

'Pa! Pa, d'you hear that? They're aiming to hang us! Hang us for something we never rightly done! You ain't gonna let them, are you?'

'Seems to me that ain't in your pa's say-so,' said Herne.

'Shut your mouth, mister!' shouted the boy. 'You done enough for one day.'

Herne was about to say something else when he noticed that the older rancher had moved down off the train steps. More than that – while his son had been shouting at him, he had managed to get his own pistol back up off the floor.

The marshal noticed Herne's silence, then the gun in the swarthy man's hand. He took a step forward, so that he could cover father and son at the same time.

'What do you think you're goin' to do with that there thing you got in your hand?'

'It's going to get us out of here. We ain't going to be hanged for something that wasn't our fault.'

He was sweating profusely and he lifted his wounded left arm across his forehead to stop it dripping down into his eyes. It could have been the moment for the marshal to have got him, Herne thought. But he was obviously going to try and talk him out of it first. He really meant what he had said about saving the town's money on ammunition.

'Look, mister, don't go off plumb loco now. All I said was that if the girl dies and if it's proved you shot her, then we'd hang you. But the way I read it, that's two ifs this side of dyin'. If I were you, I'd want to hang on to them ifs.' He chuckled out loud.

The rancher didn't seem to think it was funny. Not at all.

'This gun's enough to get us out of here. I'm telling you to back off from my boy there and put up that damned scatter gun of yours.'

The marshal looked straight back at him. He may not be all that old, thought Herne, but he's been in enough situations like this to know what to do. And he sure ain't acting scared.

'I'm telling you once more,' threatened the rancher. 'Then I'm goin' to drop you where you stand.'

The marshal didn't waste any more breath. He pulled in on both triggers. The head of the rancher's son was near enough taken off at the neck by the blast. Behind him, the rancher himself was flattened back against the steps at the end of the train carriage.

Herne watched as the man's body continued to jerk and shake for several moments as though trying to climb up on to the train of its own accord.

Eventually it gave up and slid downwards over the edge of the platform, on to the track, and ended up nestled against one of the wheels of the train.

Several feet to Herne's left, Wayne Pardoe gave a low, appreciative whistle. The rest of the people on the platform were stunned into silence. The marshal hadn't bothered to move from where he was standing. The shotgun remained in his left hand, while he drew the Remington pistol from the shoulder holster with his right.

It was with this that he now covered Herne and Pardoe.

'I guess I don't need to say any more to make my point, do I?' he asked them.

Herne could not restrain himself from grinning. 'Guess you just about said it all,' he replied.

At that point a woman started to cry loudly and conversation broke out in the crowd. The marshal turned on them angrily. 'Will you move yourselves out of here! This train ain't goin' to be leaving for a while yet. Not till I've finished sorting things out.'

The woman's sobs continued.

'One of you men, get that woman out of here! And someone else get the undertaker up here. Jackson, you and Porter get down on the track and lift that body up here. Just mind you don't slip on anything. There's a whole mess of brains all over this damned place.'

Herne stood and watched the marshal. It was a sight that both impressed him and filled him for a moment with nostalgia for his own past. Something over ten years ago that could have been him standing there giving orders so confidently and having no doubts that they would be carried out. He wondered what would happen to the young marshal in the future. If he had a future. Soon the punk gunslingers looking to make their reputations would come flocking into town. Should they miss him here they would get him in the next place or the one after that.

Unless he pulled out in time and found himself a good woman and settled down . . . like he had done himself. And what good had come of that?

'How is she, doc?' said the marshal to the man bending over the woman in a green suit, who was still lying at the far end of the platform.

The man turned his head slowly. 'She's fading good and fast. It ain't worth moving her,' he said wearily.

The marshal walked towards the huddled body, gesturing with his gun to Herne and Pardoe, indicating that they should keep ahead of him. The three of them stood around the young woman and the kneeling doctor. He had opened up the top of her green suit and had cut away a portion of the white blouse she had been wearing underneath it. He had exposed her breast.

what had been her breast. Now it was little more than raw wound, through which blood continued to pulse despite the doctor's attempts to stem the flow.

As the men looked down on her, the girl opened her eyes. Somehow, even in those moments before death, she still managed to look beautiful.

She opened her mouth in an attempt to speak. The words came haltingly. The doctor bent his head low over her lips and listened.

When she had finished, he turned his head towards the standing men. 'She asks if her fiancé is here? She was waiting for him off the train. He was bringing her a ring all the way from Denver.'

Herne and Pardoe looked at the marshal who shook his head quickly. Pardoe pulled a diamond ring from his little finger and passed it over to the doctor. 'Give her that,' he whispered.

The man accepted the ring and put it into the girl's hand. She smiled and tried to lift it up to her face so that she could look at it, but the effort was too much for her. She contented herself with holding it tight in her palm.

Then she tried to speak again. 'She says for him to kiss her,' the doctor reported.

There was a slight pause. Then Wayne Pardoe went down on his knees and lowered his head to hers. He kissed her softly and as he did so the hand that held the ring opened and let it roll down on to the boards.

The fingers were not to close again.

When Pardoe lifted his head back up, there was blood upon his lips.

The conversation between the marshal and Herne and Pardoe was brief and to the point. He checked out where they were from and where they were headed. Asked the gambler his version of the rancher's story about the cheating and seemed to accept it. After that, there was little more to say.

'One thing,' said Herne, 'I'd appreciate knowing your name.'

'Sure,' said the marshal. 'It's Dan. Dan Stewart.'

'Hell!' exclaimed Herne. 'Your old man wasn't John Stewart?'

The marshal smiled and nodded his head. 'He sure was. Still is. You knew him?'

'Rightly did. We rode together a time or two back.'

'What's your handle then?'

'Jed Herne.'

'Herne the Hunter?'

'So they say.'

Now it was the young marshal's turn to whistle. He scratched at the ground with the toe of his boot. 'If I'd known that at the time, I might not have waved this here gun at you as lightly as I did.'

Herne grinned. 'I don't know, Dan. I reckon you might have. I'm glad it didn't come to the point where we had to put anything to the test.'

'So am I! My old man would never forgive me, drawing on one of his old friends.'

Herne's mouth broke into a full smile. 'He surely wouldn't. Specially if you'd lost out!'

'What you aimin' on doing now?'

'Catching that train if it's still waiting.'

'She's there all right. You wouldn't care for a drink first?'

Herne and Pardoe exchanged glances. 'No thanks. We've tried the beer once.'

Marshal Dan Stewart laughed and held out his hand. Both men shook it warmly, then turned away and walked back to the station. The marshal watched them go, all the while thinking about what Herne had said and wondering, in spite of himself, who would have won if it had come to a showdown between them.

As for Jed Herne, he didn't give the matter more than a cursory thought. He was sure of the answer already. The day he wasn't would be the day he stopped hanging out his gun for hire.

But he was glad he had not had to shoot the son of an old friend like Long John Stewart. Long John, who had always claimed that he was born at one end of a rainbow in Omaha and would wind up being buried at the other. Long John who loved nothing better than to spend day after day up in the hills chasing down wild horses.

Herne was glad he was still alive. Somewhere. One day it would be good to ride out and meet him and talk about the old times. One day.

When he had finished his present business. When he had got rid of Nolan. Then there would be time to go visiting.

Maybe . . .

9

What was it Isaac Mellor had said to him back in Charity? Something about showing a cowboy anything that resembled civilisation and he'll do his best to try and smash it down? Well, thought Herne, I don't reckon I feel quite that bad about progress, but . . .

San Francisco wasn't as bad as New York, though there were enough solid, three or four storey buildings around to make it clear that this was no overnight sensation. This was a settled community, built on money. Money that had bought stone and brick and constructed itself a base that wouldn't easily crumble away.

Hell, thought Herne, as he looked about him, it would take an earthquake to shift this place!

'This senator of yours,' said Pardoe, 'you any idea where he is?'

'Not really. I figured that an important man like that wouldn't be all that difficult to find. Even in a town this big.'

'Unless he wants to be,' commented Pardoe.

'Meaning?'

'If he did by any chance get to hear about what happened back in New York then it's odds on that he's expecting you to come looking for him. That being so, he may have elected to disappear from sight.'

Herne shrugged. 'I'll just have to ask around.'

'Mightn't that be a mite risky. He's expecting you, then likely he's got the word out for a gunman asking questions about where he is. According to you, it seems to be his thing to hire a parcel of men to protect him and do his dirty work for him.'

Herne knew all that the gambler said was true and he told him so.

'Why don't you give me the opportunity to repay you for the very considerable favours you've done for me?'

'How's that?'

'I meet a lot of people over the cards. Gossip's a natural thing. There isn't anything much about a town you can't hear in its saloons. Not if you keep your ears open. You lie low for a while. I'll find out where Senator Nolan is.'

It sounded sensible, but Herne was feeling restless again. Impatient to be about his business. To have got all that way from one coast of the country to the other and then to have to hide up in some hotel room . . .

'It's up to you, of course, Jed. But I should appreciate being given the chance to help.'

'How long do you reckon you'll need?' Herne asked.

'Couple of days, maybe. That should be enough to get a good lead anyway.'

Herne thought about it a little longer but there was no way in which he could turn down the gambler's offer.

'All right. Two days. But after that I'm going to move around in the open and see what I can find for myself.'

The two men shook hands on the agreement. It would be two days when the time would hang heavy for Jed Herne, but after those days were over . . .

As it happened, he didn't have to wait so long. After his first evening's gambling, Wayne Pardoe came back to the small, anonymous hotel at which they were both staying. There was a twinkle in his eyes.

'You sure look as though you had luck in your corner tonight,' said Herne.

The gambler cast his eyes downwards and shook his head ostentatiously. 'Terrible!' he complained loudly. 'I do believe I lost more money this evening than at any other time in my whole career.'

'Then what are you looking so all-fired pleased about?'

'I found our man!'

'Nolan?'

'Certainly.'

Herne jumped up from the bed on which he had been lying. 'Well, come on! Where is he?' He was shouting. Excited.

'Patience, Jed, patience!'

'To hell with patience! Just tell me where he is!'

Wayne realised that it was no use stalling any longer. He told what he had discovered in as much detail as he could. 'Seems he not only doesn't want you looking for him, he doesn't want anyone else doing it either. Keeps himself shut away in a house on top of a street called Telegraph Hill. Sits in a big room all day and counts his money. Never leaves the place. Used to get out once in a while with his son, but since the boy was killed he never does that. Locks himself up in the house with enough armed men around the place to keep a small army out.'

'What's the place look like? You know that?'

'From what I was told there's a high wall, mostly covered with ivy. On the other side of that there's pretty big grounds patrolled by his men and some dogs. The house itself is built from stone. It's four storeys and his room is on the second.'

'You found out a lot,' said Herne, impressed.

'Got into a game with a feller who used to work there till he was fired. Fell asleep on guard and one of the others reported him. That was enough for Nolan.'

'Reckon you could trust what he told you?'

'I think so. He didn't have any cause to lie to me. And he sure hadn't a reason for protecting Nolan. Hated him like rattlesnake poison.'

'Fair enough.' Herne stood up and reached for his gun belt.

'You're not going there now?' exclaimed Pardoe, surprised.

'Sure am. With luck there might be another guard or two taking a sleep.'

Pardoe sighed and stood up.

'What do you think you're about to do?' asked Herne.

The gambler looked astonished. 'Go with you of course. I never thought you'd go alone.'

'You've done your part,' said Herne. 'Now it's time for mine.'

'You can't go up against all of them men alone.'

The grim smile returned to Herne's lips. 'See here, every time there's been guns around, it's me that's had to end up shooting those folks who were out to get you. Now I don't want to go after Nolan worried about having to get you out of some scrape or other. No offence, but I shall feel a whole lot easier if you're back here asleep.'

Pardoe opened his mouth to protest, but realised that it was no use. He sat down on the chair alongside the bed and watched Herne make the rest of his preparations.

It wasn't too dark and it wasn't too bright. Just an ordinary night like many another. Ordinary except for the house at the crest of the hill. Ordinary except for the man who stepped silently around it.

Nolan had amassed so much wealth that he had got himself into the position where he could not enjoy spending it. You don't get money like that without making a whole lot of enemies along with it. So you have to protect yourself – and your fortune. Almost the only thing that the senator willingly spent anything on now was protection.

He paid one hell of a lot to stop other folks taking away the money he couldn't spend.

Herne wondered how many evenings, alone in that house, the senator sat pondering over the irony of his situation.

The moon slid out into full view and Jed stopped moving, flattening himself back against the outside wall. The brickwork was rough against his fingertips – and cold. As far as he had been able to gather there were two men who made a patrol of the exterior on the quarter-hour. When they weren't doing that, the pair of them stood by the iron gates at the front of the house, hands jammed down into the pockets of their long coats, moaning and cursing the coldness and length of the night.

From what he had seen over the wall, another pair of guards walked around inside the grounds. These were the ones who had the dogs; two vicious looking German shepherds which pulled hard at their leashes they were held back on.

There was no way of knowing how many more waited inside the house itself. But likely several.

Herne regretted that there were so many. Partly for making his job that much more difficult; partly because of the necessity of killing at least some of those men. But . . . they had known what they were doing when they had taken on their jobs. Most of all, Nolan had known what he was paying them to risk. If there was an ultimate responsibility, then it was his, thought Herne, not mine. Not mine.

He drew the bayonet from his boot and started to move carefully around the outside wall. It was almost time for the two men on patrol to make their next circuit.

The shape of the wall was rectangular; Herne stood back against it by one corner. Listened for footsteps coming towards him from the right. Two men making perhaps their tenth circuit of the night. Men who were bored by their monotonous duties. Cold due to the wind that moved across the top of the hill like a sheet of ice. Wind that pierced into them as they turned corners; pierced their clothing like . . . like a knife.

Herne stepped out suddenly. His right hand drove itself into the chest of the man immediately in front of him. That hand held the bayonet blade. His left hand moved quickly up to the other guard's face. In that hand nestled the Colt, the hammer already cocked back.

The first guard bent forward, his hands reaching round the blade. Herne pushed upwards and felt something burst against the point. Then the hands fell quickly away. The guard's mouth opened and blood gushed out.

All the while – a time that was in reality brief, but which seemed to stretch on for eternity – the second guard stared down into the barrel of Herne's gun. He looked at the hammer and wanted to close his eyes but he could not. They were open as wide as they could go. As though pins had fixed them back, holding the fleshy folds of his eyelids tight against his face.

Herne tugged the bayonet clear from the man's chest and transferred the point to the neck of the guard who was still standing. He released the hammer of the Colt and moved it back across his body and down into the holster.

He spoke softly, but the man heard every word as clearly as if he was shouting. 'That could have been you. If you call out or make a wrong move, it will be. Understand?'

Eyes still unnaturally wide, the terrified man nodded.

'Right. Take that coat off him.'

Herne waited, then slipped the coat on himself. At the front there was a patch that was sticky and wet with the blood of the man from whose body it had just been removed.

'Now walk round to the gate. Easy.'

The guard did as he was told. At the wrought iron double gates, the two of them stopped.

'Key,' said Herne.

'No.'

'What the hell do you mean, no?' Herne hissed.

'We don't have the key. They let us out from inside. We have to knock to get in again.'

'What if you need to warn them of something?'

'We just holler and they come a-runnin'.'

'Hell!'

Herne had been hoping to slip in quietly with the second guard and make a try at getting right into the house alongside him. Now it seemed that it wasn't going to be possible.

'Okay. When I tell you, you let out a good shout. Tell them someone bushwacked your pal. Just get them up here and get that gate open. And don't say a damn word about me, or you'll find it's your last.'

The man looked back at Herne, a bemused expression on his face.

'What's the matter with you? You don't understand me or somethin'?'

'No, mister. I understand you.'

'That's good. You see it stays that way.'

Herne moved back away from the gate and against the wall. 'All right. Now you do as I say. And do it good.'

The guard hesitated a few moments longer. Then he grabbed tight hold of the bars of the gate and yelled out in a cracked voice. 'Help! Hey! Get down here! Someone's stabbed Jimmy. Get down here quick.'

Herne listened for voices from within, but there was no immediate activity. When he did hear them, it was obvious that they weren't being drawn to the gate right off. They appeared to be arguing about the best move to make.

'Tell them to get a move on!' whispered Herne urgently.

'Hey! Get down here fast! Jimmy's hurt real bad!'

The voices inside the darkness of the grounds became more urgent, but still no one came to the gate. Then Herne heard footsteps moving up the gravel path. One man. So that was the way they were playing it.

He held himself back and waited while the footsteps approached.

'What's going on, Al?' asked the new voice.

'I don't know. We was attacked sudden. It was over in a minute. Jimmy, he's . . . '

'He's what?' came the impatient reply.

'He's back round by the wall. He's hurt real bad.'

'Well drag him round here and we'll take him into the house.'

'Hell, Frank, you'll have to come out and give me a hand. Maybe those fellers who got him are still out there waiting.'

'Fellers? How many of them?'

'I don't know, Frank. It's too dark to see.'

There was a pause during which Herne could hear the guard shifting his boots over the gravel while he weighed up the situation. Then he called back, 'I'm comin' out, Al. I'll lock the gate behind me. You stay where you are.'

Herne heard the key turn in the lock. He held his breath as the metal catch snapped back. His eyes were fixed on the face of the guard on his side of the wall. The gate swung back and the man called Frank stepped half way out into the street.

'Where the hell did you say this happened?'

Al didn't respond.

'Well, where is he? Which way?' Frank demanded.

Fear filled the man's eyes. He didn't seem capable of speech. But neither could he prevent his eyes drifting to the point alongside the gate where Herne was standing. Eyes that gave their warning too late.

'What the . . . ?'

Frank stepped forward and looked over in the direction of Al's sly glance. At that moment Herne threw the bayonet, from very close range. The blade plunged into Al's belly. Its impact sent him juddering several yards backward. Before his body had had time to hit the ground, Herne had drawn his gun and was pointing it at Frank.

'Hold it right there!' he barked.

Frank took one look at the man standing in darkness, and decided that that was enough. 'No way!' he shouted and whirled round and ran back inside the grounds.

Why in the name of tarnation does everyone make life so difficult, thought Herne. He stood in the gateway and levelled his Colt at the shape that was rapidly becoming lost in the surrounding gloom.

He fired.

The man called Frank stopped in his tracks then crashed to the ground. He didn't move again.

Herne did. Fast. There was a clump of bushes over to the right and he dived headlong into them before anyone else appeared on the scene. Just in time . . .

'What the hell!?'

'Frank? Frank?'

'Jesus Christ!'

A number of lights had gone on in the downstairs windows. Herne waited to see if the front door would open.

'Keep calm! And turn off those damned lights!'

Almost at once, the lights went out.

Ahead of him, on the drive, Herne could just make out the silhouettes of several men pulling Frank's prostrate body towards the house.

'Whoever it was shot him in the back, the rotten bastard!'

'Don't worry. We'll get him. Bring those dogs over here.'

Herne checked his gun, tensed himself, waited.

He knew he wasn't going to like this part. He was fond of animals – more so than he was of his fellow man.

At first it seemed that the dogs had not picked up his scent but he was sure they soon would. He wondered how many of the beasts they had loosed on his trail?

In the event it turned out to be only one. He saw the large black shape bounding across the damp grass. It stopped suddenly in its tracks, raised its head, sniffed the air, then gave two loud barks. Herne steadied his gun.

The dog lowered its head and pawed the ground. It had found him. It came at him with a rush. Herne waited until it was almost on top of him, eyes bright, yellow fangs glinting in the moonlight, jaws slavering, then fired.

The dog halted in mid-air. The bullet had torn through the top of its head. It crashed into the bushes, whimpered briefly, then lay still.

Herne let out a sigh of relief and listened keenly in the cold night air. It was unlikely that his pursuers had loosed only one dog after him. There must be at least one more somewhere in the grounds. But where? He picked himself up and ran quietly over the grass, towards the side of the house. He wished he knew where the other dog was.

Suddenly he knew. It sprang from nowhere to meet him. Before Herne had a chance of getting a shot at it. He pushed up his left arm in front of his face. He yelled out in pain as the sharp teeth closed around it, biting through several layers of clothing; through skin; coming down against the bone.

The force of the dog's leap had knocked him backwards and now man and animal rolled over and over on the grass. Herne did his best to ram his arm further into the dog's mouth, forcing it wider. The beast bit down angrily, seeking to get past the outflung arm and tear at Herne's throat.

The noise spread through the grounds of the house and people soon came running. Herne used every remaining effort to throw the dog over on to its back. Then he lifted it into the air, teeth still digging into his arm like needle points of fire. He slammed the animal down on to the ground with all of his strength. The dog's grip on his left arm held. Herne crouched, drew his gun and fired into the underside of the dog's body, then smashed the butt down on its head. The sound of crunching bone could be heard clearly in the stillness of the night air.

Herne pulled his left arm clear and turned in the same movement. There were three men running towards him. Three shapes. A sudden flash and the explosion of a pistol being fired. Shouts of anger. Herne dropped to one knee and fired three times in quick succession. The nearest man threw up his arms and let out an almighty yell. Herne's shot had caught him right in the crotch.

He had winged one of the others; missed the third. Not that he had waited around to count. He figured now was time to get inside the house.

As his boots hit the grit of the drive, running hard, there was a sudden blaze of light as the massive front door was thrown open. Herne saw the sharp outline of a man holding a rifle. He raised his Colt and fired as he ran.

The man fell backwards into the light. Almost, for a moment, as though he was wearing a halo. Herne jumped through the door and stared around. Apart from the sprawled figure of the dead man and his weapon the only thing he noticed immediately was an oil lamp hanging in the centre of the hallway. Herne swivelled round at the sound of men racing towards him. Realising that the light made him a prime target, he flattened himself fast, snapping off a shot as he did so. The men still came forward. Herne nestled behind the cover of the dead man's body and rested his gun arm against it. Two shots. Two more dead bodies.

Quickly he got up and slammed the heavy wooden door shut. Leaning back against it, he drew his breath in gasps through thinly parted lips. He reloaded his Colt and revolved the chamber. To the right of the hallway, stairs climbed up at an angle. On either side were closed doors.

Herne cursed the sheer size of the house and wondered how many men waited in hiding behind its closed doors. Wondered behind which one of them he would discover Senator Nolan.

He decided that the only thing to do was to start on the ground floor and work upwards, checking a room a time. In the kitchen he dragged a terrified Chinese by his pigtail out from behind a cupboard. But the little man was too numb with fear to help him in any way. Herne left him cringing on the stone floor and moved on.

Dining rooms, guest rooms, bedrooms: all empty, save one which contained a silver haired cat. It jumped from off a silk bed cover and ran purring around his feet, seeking to be stroked.

Herne nudged it away with the side of his boot. He didn't have much time for cats. Especially aristocratic looking ones like that. Right now he had no time for anything.

He hesitated outside a double-doored room on the second floor. Thought he heard a movement inside. Drew his gun and placed his left hand upon one of the door handles. Pulled it down towards himself and stepped in quickly.

The room was lit by a low-burning lamp. The remains of a log fire smouldered in the hearth. In the centre of the room a large chair was placed with its high back to the door. From the other side of the chair a narrow strand of cigar smoke curled upwards to the ceiling.

Herne took several paces forward, gun at the ready.

'Take it real easy. Get up out of that thing and face this way. And keep your hands high,' he ordered.

Almost immediately, the chair began to swivel round upon its base. Herne watched, fascinated. A figure spun slowly into view. A blanket draped across the knees. In the left hand a cigar that was three parts smoked down. Herne stared at the face. It wasn't right. It wasn't right!

'Don't move, cowboy!'

The voice had come from behind him. Herne froze.

'Let that gun of yours drop to the floor.'

Herne hesitated.

'Drop it or I'll blow a hole in you big enough to put a fist right through!'

Herne's fingers loosed their grip. The Colt dropped on to the carpet.

'That's good.'

Herne watched as the man in the chair in front of him withdrew his right hand from underneath the blanket. In it was a cocked pistol. The smile that crept over the man's face changed into a laugh which twisted the right side of his mouth.

He stood up and flung the blanket down on to the floor. 'Get his gun,' he said to the man behind Herne. A hand picked the weapon up from off the dark red carpet.

'Surprised, cowboy?'

Herne looked back at him but said nothing.

'See, that ain't my chair. It's usually the old man who's wrapped up under that blanket. But he's long gone, leaving us here behind him. Waiting for any visitors who might come in out of the night.' He looked arrogantly at Herne, his face contorting once more. 'I'll say this for you, though, cowboy, you were better than I thought you'd be. Heh, regular Billy the Kid, ain't he?'

His companion chuckled agreement.

'Anyway. You'll get what you wanted. You'll get to see the old man right enough. We got orders. We'll tie you up and keep you till he gets back. Even tend to that arm of yours. Make certain you don't die of rabies or something like that. The old man wants to look at you. Only then will we be able to kill you. And after what you did tonight, that sure is going to be a pleasure.'

Still Herne didn't answer. He was busy weighing up his chances. Deciding that they didn't look any too good. Two men held guns on him and they looked as though they knew only too well how to use them. It was their trade. Just like it was his. Only at that moment, they were holding all the aces . . .

Something jogged in his brain, something . . .

He heard, or thought he heard, a footstep on the stairs. Someone climbing up cautiously, carefully. Someone who didn't want his presence to be known.

'Damn it!' Herne suddenly shouted out. 'This arm of mine's hurting like merry hell. Can't you do something for it?'

'Sure, cowboy,' said the one who had taken him from behind. 'Sure we can. Let's see that poor old arm of yours.'

He took a step towards Herne, then lashed out with the barrel of the gun he was holding. He ground it hard into the wound that the dog's teeth had made, causing Herne to wince with the pain.

He stepped back and laughed in Herne's face. 'How d'you like that, cowboy?' he sneered.

Herne held his left arm. Other than that he didn't answer. He didn't have to. Someone else answered for him. Wayne

Pardoe. Pardoe who had been making his way silently up the stairs and along the corridor to the open doorway.

He answered by twice firing the gun he was holding into the jeering man's back. Instantly, Herne dived at the second man, hands clawing for the pistol. Finding it. Feeling the cold metal against his hand. Forcing it back and up.

A knee rammed itself upwards and Herne was forced to loose his grip. For a second the gun moved free. Then Herne threw a punch at the man's jaw which connected with enough force to drive him over towards the wall.

'Duck, Jed!'

Pardoe's shout was loud and clear. Herne didn't hesitate. He ducked. The shot blasted out in the room and over by the fire the oil lamp flickered crazily. The man's body was hammered back into the wall once more. Only this time the blow was lethal. Fingers found the wound and the right side of the face twisted upwards. He died with that lunatic attempt at a smile on his face.

Wayne Pardoe walked over to Herne who was picking himself up from the carpet. 'Thought I'd try to pay off the rest of my debt,' he said.

'Plumb glad you did,' admitted Herne.

'Besides, all those remarks about my prowess with a gun were beginning to hurt enough for me to believe they were true.'

Herne looked at the Colt .44 in the gambler's hand. 'I'd only seen you with that little toy derringer of yours before. Never did see you handle a real gun.'

'Trouble with these things,' said Pardoe with a half-smile, 'is they make unsightly bulges in your suits. Now I'm a man who sets great store by appearances . . . which reminds me, I believe this is your property.'

He reached inside his coat and drew from his belt the bayonet blade. 'I found this outside the gate and just followed the trail of dead bodies until I found you. What are you doing anyway? Staging another Battle of the Little Big Horn?'

He laughed at his own joke. In the middle of the laugh a gun shot choked it short. Wayne Pardoe fell forward into Herne's arms with an open-mouthed expression of wonder.

Herne looked over the slumped head at the wounded man on the floor. The one they had taken for dead when two of the gambler's shells had ploughed into his back.

They had been wrong.

Herne watched as the man attempted to shift the gun to take aim at himself. But the effort was too much. He saw the gun slip forward, then revolve around the man's finger as it stayed within the guard. His head banged against the floor with a thud that was dulled by the thickness of the carpet.

Herne laid Pardoe down gently. Not that it mattered. If he'd dropped him from his full height, he would never have noticed. Herne closed his eyes for an instant. Pardoe had proved to be a good friend. Only he should have stuck to playing poker. It brought him better luck.

A low moan returned Herne's attention to the wounded man on the floor. Herne went over and knelt beside him. Pardoe's bullets had both penetrated through to the front. The man didn't have long to go . . . and there were questions that wanted answering.

Herne propped up the guard's head. 'All right. Where is he? Where's Nolan?'

The man opened his mouth and coughed; a snake of blood slithered slowly over his lower lip and down on to his chin.

'Where's Nolan?'

'I . . . I . . . I ain't tellin'.'

Herne grabbed hold of him and shook him hard. 'I ain't bin through all this for another damned dead end. You tell me where he is or it'll be the worse for you.'

The fading eyes sought Herne's. 'It ain't no good threatenin' me. I know I'm gonna die anyhow.'

Herne drew the bayonet from his boot. The blade that Wayne Pardoe had returned to him. He lifted up the man's hand and held it in front of his face.

'Open your eyes and look, damn you!'

The man opened his eyes and watched horror-struck as Herne cut off his little finger.

'Christ! You bastard! You fuckin' mad bastard!' he croaked.

Herne held the man's hand tightly as the blood ran down

over his own fingers, pulsing out of the open wound in tiny spurts.

'You may not have long to live, but I reckon you got long enough for me to take off every finger on this hand. And then the other one. After that maybe we can find a few other things to cut away. You ain't goin' to like that.'

'You . . . you wouldn't . . . '

Herne sliced away the next finger.

The man stared wide-eyed, then turned his head to one side as vomit forced its way through his throat. He coughed and gagged and seemed about to choke. Herne hit him high on the back and he shrieked aloud. He spat a mouthful of blood out on to the already red carpet.

'Where the fuck is Nolan?'

Herne once more moved the razor sharp blade towards the man's hand.

'No! I'll . . . tell . . . you.'

And he did. Herne listened carefully, having to bend his head so low to catch the words that his face was splashed with the bubbles of red that burst from the dying man's lips as he spoke.

Then, when he had heard everything, he swiftly drew the bayonet across the man's throat from ear to ear. Jed Herne wasn't the sort of person who liked anyone to suffer unnecessarily.

10

It was not only during the nights that San Francisco was damp in January. In daylight hours too, when the white clouds of mist came rolling in from the bay, the clawing wetness sought out everything, everyone.

So that, when it became too bad, those who could sought escape. And as he sought to escape from the vengeance of Herne the Hunter, in the same way Senator Nolan attempted to flee the atmosphere of the city.

He bought his way out.

Nolan had chartered a special railroad car to take him up into the hills that surrounded the city. There the air would be cleaner, calmer – more restful.

Jed Herne rode along at a leisurely pace. The sky above was still overcast, but the temperature had risen considerably. He found it good to be in the saddle again, enjoying the rhythmic movement of the animal beneath him. Good to be on the trail again.

Especially as he knew that this time there would be gold at the rainbow's end. For above him, ahead of him, the senator's train was slowly making its way. As long as Herne keep in sight of the rail track he was content. He would catch up with the senator soon enough. And then . . .

Money. Hell! thought Herne. Money was a kind of cancer that spread through the bloodlines of certain families and made them rotten. He remembered the Stanwyck woman and her two sons, hidden away in a place that was built like a fortress. Built out of money. Innocent from the outside but rotten inside.

Like opening up a crisp green apple and finding its core diseased, crawling with maggots. Herne shuddered.

Trains. It had all begun with a train. A specially chartered train – the one that the senator's son had hired to carry himself and several ill-assorted companions on a gambling jaunt across country. No chance of an interruption that way; they could drink and play cards to their hearts' content. Nolan had the money that made it possible, so why not? Trains and money.

Herne visualised the over-confident, spoiled face of Josiah Nolan. Imagined him rubbing his well-manicured hands together with anticipation, a puffy smile on his thin, mean-looking lips. In anticipation of making a killing!

And so he had. Though almost certainly not the one he had had in mind. Not even one. Two. Two women. One of them Jed's. He looked up at the vast greyness of the sky as it stretched from one distant horizon to the other. In all of that space he could see nothing but the figure of a young woman wearing her best dress. A dress that was beginning to spread round her belly with the first visible signs of pregnancy. She had only worn it once, that green velvet dress. For a special occasion.

Like hanging herself when she knew that she could not hope to live with the memory of what had happened to her.

She had died before Jed had woken and found her. Her memory had not. It lived on inside Herne himself. Lived and drove him. Onwards. Upwards.

Herne shook his head in an attempt to dispel his sudden gloom. This time no spectre hovered in the sky. Just grey clouds. And away from him stretched the black lines of the railroad track.

He clicked gently to his horse and touched her flanks with his spurs.

'Come on, now. We've got things to do. Let's climb a little.'

An hour later Herne saw the train. There were only two cars being pulled behind the engine. He urged his mount harder, moving in closer with every pace.

Soon he could distinguish the rear car. The blinds were pulled down against the light – such as there was. Apparently,

Senator Nolan chose to spend most of his time in comparative darkness. Chose to . . . or had to.

Herne had found that out from the guard back at the house in San Francisco before he had killed him. Also, that the senator would be accompanied in the blacked-out carriage by his two top bodyguards. Men to whom Nolan paid a small fortune. For theirs was the final responsibility.

He had not learnt much about them. Only their names: Neilson and Lamont. And the fact that Lamont was a negro. The dying man had thought that would interest Herne, but Jed couldn't see why.

When you were going to kill a man, what the hell did the colour of his skin matter?

There was a point up ahead of him where the track wound itself alongside a small stream. Both water and rail moved in close to a fairly steep bluff. Herne reined in and looked thoughtful; then he pushed his horse back into motion. Wheeling round to the east. Fast.

Now he knew what he should do.

He left the animal tucked out of sight over the incline, tying her to the overhanging branch of a tree. Then he hurried down the side of the bluff, leaning back against it so as not to lose his balance. Boots digging into the hard ground to find footing. Hands now steadying, now pushing him on his descent.

Finally he slithered to a halt at a point that was almost directly above where the train would pass. Below him, the stream coursed strongly, the recent rain having nearly swollen it over its banks.

All around, the landscape was bleak, dead-looking.

Into this deadness, moved the train. The steam that emerged darkly from its engine funnel soon became one with the sky.

Train of death.

Herne steadied himself and checked quickly that the leather tag was pulled up from the back of his holster over the hammer of his gun. He didn't want that to shake free when he dropped downwards.

He held himself back against the sloping ground as the engine passed below him. The driver and his fireman were busy with their tasks. Neither looked up. After all, on such a drab day, what could there possibly be to look at?

Herne pushed himself forward, timing his jump so that he would miss the tender and land on top of the first, hopefully empty, car. He tensed himself and then relaxed as the jolt of the impact thrust up through his legs.

He immediately flattened himself on top of the car. Looked round anxiously towards the engine. No one moved. The sound must have been lost in the noise from the moving train. He waited a few moments longer. Partly to get his breath back. Partly for the terrain to level out. He didn't want the rear car to go rolling back down hill. Not with him on it, he didn't.

Ready now, Herne crawled along to the end of the carriage and climbed down off the roof. The door that led into the senator's car was firmly closed. Herne bent down and lowered both of his arms underneath the iron coupling hook which held the carriages together.

The occasional bumping of the wheels on the somewhat uneven track did not make his task easier. It was some time before he was able to drag the hook clear of its linkage. He knew that his forearms would be bruised and there was a troubling ache from the injured left arm where the dog had savaged it.

Herne jumped free from the still moving section and leapt upon the almost stationary carriage. His right hand loosed the tag from the hammer of his Colt; the left went to the handle of the door. Tested it. It did not budge more than a fraction of an inch. And it would not be long before those inside realised that something had gone wrong. That they had stopped moving.

Which was fine. Because it meant that sooner or later one of those who were within the darkened car would have to look out and see what had happened. A window would open. Or a door.

Herne ran on to the grass at the side of the track, putting some space between himself and the carriage.

Herne crouched down and surveyed the drawn blinds. He could only see one side, of course, with a good view of the observation platform at the back and a partial view of the shorter section that led away from the front end.

He waited and waited. Nothing happened. The water continued to flow down towards the bay; the clouds moved relentlessly by overhead. Other than that there was no movement. No sound.

They must have realised what had happened. So why were they waiting? Supposing it was 'they' . . . It was always possible that the man back at the house had lied to him. But, when Herne recalled his terror-stricken face, he could scarcely believe that to be true. His information might simply have been wrong. The senator could have been in the forward carriage – no, he would have seen signs of movement through the windows. Or perhaps he was not on the train at all?

The thoughts raced through Jed Herne's mind as he continued to watch the train like a hawk staring down on its prey.

He could only guess that if his information were correct and Nolan and the two bodyguards were inside, then they must have assumed that it was an attempt to either assassinate or kidnap the senator, being carried out by more than one man.

They were probably sitting in the car envisaging armed men surrounding the train on either side.

Well, Herne grinned, let them sweat it out. I ain't in any hurry. Not now I've got this far.

He had little fears of interference from other quarters. He did not think that the driver and fireman of the train would want to become involved in whatever strange events were taking place back along the track. They would probably pretend they hadn't noticed anything was wrong and just keep on going.

Which, thought Herne as he stared downwards, just leaves me and you.

At which point he held his breath.

His eye had picked up a movement low on the ground on the far side of the stranded car. Surely? Yes. There it was again. Something shifting slowly, surreptitiously along behind the wheels.

One of the men had managed to slide through a window on the blind side and was now trying to make his way to the rear end of the car without being spotted.

Fine, thought Herne. Let him keep on thinking he's doing just that.

The man was edging his way along with such patience that it was almost possible to believe there was no one there at all. Whoever he was, he was not going to be easy. He knew what he was doing.

Herne wondered if it was Neilson or Lamont. White or black. It was idle speculation as it didn't really matter. At least, not to Herne. It might conceivably matter to Lamont or Neilson.

Whichever of the two it turned out to be was five feet away from the observation platform. Herne drew his Colt and crooked his arm at the elbow, resting it upon his knee. He lowered his head behind the hammer and, with one eye closed, sighted along the barrel.

The man would have noticed that there was nobody on the stream side. Which probably meant he expected to find a whole gang round the side where Herne was waiting. Patiently. As patiently as the gunman who had that second eased his left boot up onto the metal floor of the rear platform. A hand pulled upwards. The right boot joined the left boot. The body swung gracefully under the rail then took up as little space as possible against the carriage end. Began to shift across to the other side. Inch by slow inch.

And still Herne waited for the first clear sign, the first target.

There was a blur of dark brown. The sleeve of a shirt? Uncertain, his finger remained poised on the trigger. Come on, damn you, said Herne to himself. Stop being so goddamn worried!

As if hearing him, the owner of the shirt obliged by showing his whole arm. Still Herne wanted more. Wanted the man's head to peer round the end of the car, so that...

The click was slight but in the intensity of all that expectant silence it sounded as loud as a hammer blow.

Christ!

Herne cussed inwardly as he flung himself to his left with all the strength he could muster. The bullet hammered into the heel of his boot, wrenching it off. Herne kept rolling.

'Christ!' he repeated, out loud this time. The other man

had gone along the far end of the train. The first had just been a decoy.

Shots now came at him from both directions, missing him as he thumped down towards the track. Suddenly he dug his feet in hard and pulled up short. Fired first at the observation platform, then, immediately after, at the other end of the car. He stood up. A searing pain shot through the back of his left calf as a bullet ripped through the skin. He looked up and saw the man furthest away duck back from sight.

Herne himself fell to the right away from the anticipated shot from the brown-shirted man on the platform. Dropped. Rolled. Came up firing. Twice. One miss. One shot that sent the man toppling back against the rail, clutching at his right thigh. He bounced backwards and Herne's next shot whistled over his head.

Then Jed was pushed back against the side of the carriage and reloading fast while there were seconds of time.

'Lamont! You all right?' The gunman nearest to Herne yelled down to the other end.

After a moment, Neilson got his answer. 'Great! How about you?'

'The bastard got me in the leg, but I'm okay.'

'Which leg was that?' laughed Lamont.

Jesus, thought Herne, as he pushed the last cartridge home, what a hell of a time to be making jokes.

The wounded man thought much the same. 'What are you cackling at, you black bastard? This ain't no laughin' matter!'

'Don't worry,' came the reply. 'There's still two of us and only one of him.'

'Goddamn it!' Neilson screamed. 'Shut your mouth and do something about gunning this feller down. You black bastard!'

Herne wondered whether Lamont was grinning or not. Then he wondered whether he was still where he had been a moment ago. Someone who was clever enough to set Herne up the way he had, getting him to concentrate on one place to the exclusion of the others – he was going to have more tricks than one.

Like setting up a conversation which would fix the positions of himself and his partner firmly in Herne's mind.

Jed holstered the gun and turned fast. He grabbed at the

ledge at the side of the train and pulled himself up. He wanted to be on that car roof and quickly. Before it was too late for him to move anywhere.

His head and shoulders were above the level of the top of the carriage for a split second. It was enough. Enough to see the smiling face of the gunman as he stepped cat-like along the centre. Lamont snapped off a shot too quickly for the aim to be good, although it was close enough for Herne to feel the wind of it as it passed by him.

Holy shit! They were good all right.

He dropped back to the ground and turned right, beginning to run for the end of the train car that Lamont had left.

'Hold it!'

He ducked low and kept running. The bullet whined into the side of the train and ricocheted away into the distance. Herne stopped sharply and turned, drawing as he did so. Neilson steadied himself for his second shot. He wasn't going to miss this time. Not now his man was standing still.

Which was exactly what Herne was thinking.

He fired fast. Two shots blurred together as though they had come from a single pull of the trigger. Neilson threw his right arm high into the air and his gun fired uselessly upwards into the grey clouds. He stumbled two paces backwards, then recovered his balance and came forward once more.

His gun arm was lowered again; he struggled desperately to level it in Herne's direction. His eyes began to blink then his arm began to droop. He fought against it. Fought hard. Lost.

The gun slipped out of still grasping fingers. Head went back, mouth and eyes open wide. Two blotches of red stained the brown shirt, less than an inch or two apart. Even as Herne watched the marks widened into one solid bloodied patch.

His legs began to separate, as though he had decided to perform the splits. Halfway through the action, the upper half of his body collapsed forwards. Finally he lay stretched out alongside the track.

Herne was moving gradually around the carriage. The black bodyguard was nowhere to be seen. He had gone back inside. Now that he was down to a one to one situation, it was the obvious thing to do.

It left Herne in the worse position: of having to come in from the light into the dark. In from the cold.

All right, thought Herne. You still don't know which entrance to watch. Which door. Which window.

He moved swiftly from one end of the car to the other, shooting off the locks of the doors as he went. But he did not make any attempt to enter. That way Lamont would be forced to check both ways at once.

Next he fired through a central pair of windows, shattering the glass and tearing back the blinds.

Herne reloaded his Colt and moved silently along to the observation platform. He prepared to kick the door open. Counted under his breath. One. Two. Three.

Kicked. The door flew open and almost instantly two shots rang out. Herne dived low, keeping himself as close to the floor as he could. The light from the doorway penetrated deep into the car. But not deep enough for him to see clearly.

He pushed himself into a gap between a pair of upholstered seats at his right and peered over them. A shot tore out of the blackness at him. He fired back. Heard an urgent shout and curse. Fired again, aiming for the source of sound.

He jumped for the other side of the gangway. But Lamont was not concerned with getting back at him. Not now. He was too intent on getting away, out of the carriage.

Three-quarters of the way down the car a blind was suddenly ripped back from one of the windows and a body went crashing through it, head first. Herne turned and ran for the open door, swinging himself over the rail that ran round the platform.

He landed at the edge of the track, alongside the bank of the stream. Lamont had made it into the water and was trying to swim across to the far side. But it looked as though one of his arms was out of action and he was not finding the going easy.

Herne decided he could wait. Again. This time it would be all right.

The black gunslinger pulled himself up the bank at the far side of the stream. He shook his head, wincing as the pain high in his side struck him afresh with the effort he had made, then turned to see where Herne was.

The flash from Herne's Colt showed him what he didn't really want to know. His eyes remained on Herne for a full ten seconds but they showed neither feeling nor expression. And at the end of that time he fell face first down into the water.

Herne watched as the current edged him away from the bank and began to move him downstream. The water around him was etched with thin red lines.

'So long,' said Herne. 'You poor black bastard.'

He turned back into the carriage. Gun still held expectantly in his right hand. He ripped the blinds down from the windows as he passed along the corridor.

Then he saw him. The man he had been searching for. The man he had come hundreds of miles with the express purpose of killing.

Senator Nolan.

He was sitting in a specially padded seat close to the centre of the car. It was made in soft, quilted velvet. Black velvet, like everything else in the carriage. The blinds. The upholstery. The hangings.

Herne put up his gun and went over to where the man sat. Stared at the face. Puffy-white, flabby, lifeless. His mouth was set. His eyes failed to move, not even a flicker. His whole head resembled a decaying vegetable. Inhuman. At the side of his neck the muscles were pulled tight as though gripped in some form of paralysis.

He had evidently suffered some kind of crippling stroke. Whatever he now was . . . this thing that surrounded itself with darkness.

There had been many things Herne had wanted to say to Nolan. He had wanted to talk about hate and revenge. About fathers and children. About his child, dead inside his wife's raped and hanged body. He had wanted to hear Nolan plead for mercy. Plead passionately for the mercy he could never allow him. Then he would kill him.

But now . . .

The part of Nolan that had been a mouth suddenly moved, parted wider. Herne lowered his face towards it. He almost reeled back at the sickly sweet smell that greeted him, that hung over Nolan's body like a cloak. The skin of his face looked as though it was a soft covering for a swollen balloon of pus. He watched as the hole in the middle of it formed two silent words: 'Kill me.'

Herne stood up and walked out on to the observation platform. Behind him something scraped against the top of the roof. He whirled round, Colt in hand. It was a vulture clawing at the metal as it took a brief respite from feeding on the exposed face of Neilson's dead body. Herne looked and saw other birds stripping away the clothing above the wounds on the dead man's chest and thigh.

He turned away from them and suddenly thought of Becky, waving down to him from the ship that had carried her away. He knew that as long as he lived nothing could be allowed to happen to her. She was the last remnant of his past, of his future. He could not afford to take a single risk.

Herne went back into the railroad car.

Moments later a shot echoed outwards. The huge birds rose, disturbed by the sudden sound. They wheeled and circled in the sky. Beyond their ugly, ominous shapes a single streak of blue showed through the grey.

THE END

BELL OF DEATH by LOUIS MASTERSON

Morgan Kane was cooling his heels in the forests of California with nothin' more pressing on his time that to catch himself a grizzly. But then he met up with a darn fool bunch of greenhorns on the trail of some long lost Aztec gold, and Kane's holiday turned into a deadly treasure hunt . . . a hunt that was shared by a savage band of escaped prisoners who'd shoot anyone who got in their way – child, woman, or U.S. Marshal. . . .

0 552 10257 1 – 45p

THE DEMON FROM NICARAGUA by LOUIS MASTERSON

Kane was a U.S. Marshal again. Six months after he'd thrown down his badge and quit, he was back – but only for a trial period. Old friends at Fort Leavenworth saw this was a new Kane: harsher, and more brutal even than before – and they gave him just one chance to prove himself. . . .

Kane hardly knew where Nicaragua was – some damn fool country in central America, he figured – but that was where they were sending him. And when he got there, he began to feel kinda easier in his mind: in that steamy country, he could smell death in the air. . . .

0 552 10331 4 – 45p